BBC National Short Story Award 2008

BBC National Short Story Award

✳ SHORT BOOKS

First published in 2008 by

Short Books

3A Exmouth House

Pine Street

EC1R 0JH

10 9 8 7 6 5 4 3 2 1

A CIP catalogue record for this book
is available from the British Library.

ISBN 978-1-906021-60-3

Contents

Preface

"FROM ITS FAÇADE the eighteenth century townhouse was indistinguishable from its terraced neighbours. The first visitor that morning betrayed no sense of the ordeal which lay ahead as she passed by the railings of the square. Before mounting the steps, she paused a moment to hear the laughter of the children playing in the communal gardens. How long would it be before she heard such unforced joy again? Once inside, there was no possibility of retreat. One by one the others joined her around the circular table, the tension in their faces reflected in the polished surface. The slaughter was about to begin."

Given those efforts of mine at fictionalising our first meeting, it is probably just as well I am a judge of the short story competition rather than an entrant, but I don't think the word "slaughter" is too far off the mark. Judging a literary contest even in the genteel surroundings of Lincoln's Inn Fields is more akin to a cull than a polite discussion. The most brutal elimination happened before we five judges began our task. Over six hundred stories are cut down to around fifty to be read by the five judges: Naomi Alderson, Alex Linklater, Penelope Lively, Di Speirs and myself. Then began the anguish as delicately wrought stories, some written by very famous authors are tossed into a reject pile. Intense discussion followed as judges lost some of their choices until the final shortlist was established through a baroque voting system handed down from previous years, said to be used by the Prix Goncourt.

Our shortlist of five is a very strong and varied one. Our first story has an arresting title: "Guidelines for Measures to Deal with Disgraceful and Other Events". Richard Beard has written four novels as well as rugby columns for *The Times*. He now lives in France, having spent time in Somerset and Hong Kong. His story has a highly inventive structure which reveals new narrative layers throughout. We felt it was exuberant and highly contemporary.

Jane Gardam is the best known writer on our list. Her novels and short story collections have been highly acclaimed. In 'The People on Privlege Hill', Jane Gardam returns to the protagonist of her novel of 2004, *Old Filth,* but this is a perfectly self contained story, a beautifully judged comedy of manners touched with poignancy.

Erin Soros, the author of 'Surge', was born and raised in Vancouver and has won many literary prizes in Canada. Her story, with its terrifying centrepiece of young children climbing a lookout tower, created a stomach churning sense of tension. The taut writing created a strong sense of place.

'The Names' was one of the stories which stood out from the very beginning. Its author Adam Thorpe is a poet, playwright and novelist who lives in France, having grown up in India, Cameroon and England. We thought it was hugely atmospheric – a clever mesh between the narrator's contemporary story and secrets of wartime France.

Our final author, Clare Wigfall, was born in London and grew up in California. Her ability (especially as a non-Scot) to recreate a tiny Gaelic-speaking island community in 'The Numbers' impressed the judges. She achieved that rare quality in a short story of capturing the past in an authentic way. One judge called it "an astonishing feat of historical ventriloquism".

I found the process of reading all the entries a genuine pleasure. I have enjoyed short stories through most of my life beginning with Saki and J.D. Salinger at school, then Isaac Bashevis Singer, Flannery O'Connor and so many others. There was immense variety in competition submissions with many younger writers entering as well as more established names. Going through this year's stories I found some bizarre points of concurrence. What is it in the zeitgeist that made at least three of the authors write about the Sami people of Finland or drove others to choose the Fens or pick the Hindu goddess Kumari as a theme?

Overall we felt that there was a polarisation in the entries with true excellence at the top of the field and then a drop in quality. Too many of the stories felt like compressed novels. Others had strived too hard for "the big ending" or predictable twist in the tale. The perfect short story arrests the reader's attention immediately and then illuminates an entire life through one scene or a few actions.

James Lasdun, the winner of the Award in its first year, has this to say about the form:

> A really great short story has more in common with poetry than the novel. It's an art of economy and exclusion, with no tolerance for digression. As in poetry the basic units of thought are the word and the image. The expansiveness that gives a novel its power is usually death to the short story.

The master of the short story Anton Chekhov boasted of being able to turn any subject into a story. His friend and fellow writer Vladimir Korolenko recorded in his memoirs that when asked how he wrote his stories, Chekhov laughed, snatched up the nearest object, an ashtray, and said that if Korolenko wanted a story called 'The Ashtray', he could have it by the next morning. At the start of his writing career Chekhov wrote short stories to make money to support his family and to pay for his medical training. His daily sketches of contemporary Russian life appeared, often under pseudonyms, in the weekly magazines of Moscow.

It seems so strange in Britain's current literary climate the short story was once regarded as a cash cow. Nowadays there is a commercial prejudice against the short story. Publishers far prefer young writers to produce a novel. Unlike the United States, there are few magazines in which short stories are published (*Prospect* being an honourable exception). New writers aren't encouraged to write short stories nor do they benefit from specialised editing in order to develop their understanding of the form.

The BBC, as the largest short story commissioner in the UK, is sponsoring the BBC National Short Story Award as a way of eroding that prejudice. We hope that readers and listeners will be encouraged to embrace the short story once more. The greater number of entries this year is perhaps an indication that the prize is working in that aim. In an era where people constantly complain about time poverty and a fast food approach to culture, what could be a more enjoyable way of consuming fiction in the 21st century than devouring a short story in one gulp?

Martha Kearney

Guidelines for Measures to Cope with Disgraceful and Other Events
Richard Beard

1. Denial

MAKE IT UNRESERVEDLY clear, as an elected member of the European Parliament, that nothing shameful could possibly have taken place. Rumours must be dismissed as unfounded and malicious, as per approved guidelines for measures to cope with disgraceful and other events.

You could, for example, deny using your office expense allowance to set up a Russian citizen with no work permit in a studio apartment on the Quai Rouget de Lisle in Strasbourg (which does not, because you have never been there, smell intensely of incense and pillows). You have never slipped across the river between midday resolutions and an afternoon meeting of the All-Party Committee Against Corruption. If necessary, you can swear this on your wife and children.

Hugh, I believe, who is six, and four-year-old Madeleine with her collection of Britannia zoo animals.

Your family isn't perfect, deny that too. Always deny perfection. Hugh didn't get on with his school in Brussels, so Georgia took the children back to Kensington the Vale in London, where thirty years ago she wore precisely the same brown uniform and straw hat with ribbon. In a family context, you can sometimes be unreasonable. 'Nobody leaves this house until I find my sock!' That was one of yours – the gang in the van had a good laugh at that one – but you public figures are often baffled at home. Nevertheless, you would not knowingly jeopardise the muddled rough-and-tumble of normal domestic life. Deny it.

You are, however, a politician. You can see every side. You can see that your enemies and the opposition and your father-in-law and the press would love any accusation of this kind to be true, which of course it isn't. Especially just now, with your eyes on a seat at the big boys' table at Westminster.

Seven years ago, in your first week in Brussels as a Euro MP, the leader of the Socialist group, Lars Knudsen, took you aside. He wanted to offer advice, to show that he knew best. He taught you how to re-serve the better tables at Comme Chez Soi, and how to get selected by BBC News 24 for interviews in the lobby. Useful stuff, and you humoured Herr Knudsen, didn't you? Cosy up in the Members' bar and talk about absolutely everything. Women and ambition.

'This is no place to be weak, Simon.'

That was the only warning he had for you, and you laughed at him behind his back. Second-rater. Wouldn't be in Brussels otherwise, but in Copenhagen. Just like you thought you ought to be in London. It was a shame about Knudsen though. I'm not sure he deserved to be sent home in disgrace, not simply for putting his personal dentist on the Weights and Measures payroll.

Procedures have been tightening up, as you know. This is probably not the best time to be seeing a young lady called Eva Kuznetsova, who is undoubtedly pretty but has no visible means of support. You should deny that you share her flat for the four days a month the Parliament sits in Strasbourg, and state firmly that you do not skim your living allowance to put Eva on the direct train to Brussels at least once a week at all other times. This is a damaging and false accusation likely to hurt your career, your wife, and your children.

Unfortunately, Denial may fail to contain events. For this measure to work, you will need a spotless reputation. You should never have associated with parliamentarians already disgraced, nor have failed to declare a non-executive directorship with a Black Sea mining company. There should be no blokey stories, however amusing, about you and female delegates in the days when you were president of the Union of European Students. Even if you yourself encouraged these stories because that was long before you were married, and in any case the girls were foreign and total Euro stun-guns. Your very own words, Simon, I do believe.

You are a politician. Denial is precarious. Most people with whom you interact, including journalists, other politicians and occasionally your own wife, are a cynical bunch who will assume that the opposite of what you say may well be true. Before risking a straight denial, you should explore other possible measures.

2. Concealment/Continued Deception

This often appears an attractive solution; it worked well enough until now. It is a legitimate way of coping with an event that might otherwise become disgraceful, like Eva Kuznetsova on the Quai Rouget de Lisle, who since last Thursday thinks she might be pregnant.

Cunning will be required. Continued deception demands a cleverness that gets increasingly stretched as time goes by. Imagine hiding a mistress and her baby. Your baby. A second family.

It was a junior minister in the Lord Chancellor's Department, on a recent visit to the Commissioner in Brussels, who singled you out at lunch and said:

'You are a very clever operator, Simon. I like that in a young man. We enjoy the way you work.'

So busy, so committed, talking shop and stopping overnight in Rome, Barcelona, Dublin, Amsterdam, every destination by happy coincidence also served by Ryanair from the Baden Airpark near Strasbourg. If you say you're going to Rome, Simon, just as you have until now, you should go, where your wife and your agent and the BBC and the whips can ring you on a genuine Rome number. If it happens that Eva is also in Rome on a 0.01 euro Ryanair flight, on the same weekend, in the same hotel, in the same room, then truly the light doth shine. As with any lie, make most of it true. Do some business. Talk to at least one German civil servant — they're impeccable as alibis. Easy. Easy-peasy for a slick cocksure bastard like you. Pardon my French.

Simon.

Here's a favourite of yours — a sly technique you should retain. Buy open-ended air tickets and then monitor the flights back to London or Brussels. Find one that's cancelled and then immediately e-mail your wife (cc the secretary) to say this is the flight you booked. They should check the arrival time on the Internet. A little later, when they make the urgent call to tell you the bad news, and you're lying in your towelling robe on a king-size bed in the Hotel Barbarini on the Via Rasella, it's clear that a delay like this is going to be hell for everybody.

Sport is good, golf best. Off for 18 holes at the Royal Waterloo or the Kempferhof but only play nine.

Swimming has good margins for creative time-keeping; triathlon training is almost foolproof.

The problem with strategies and deception, as you know, is cash-flow. It costs to be clever, and for these purposes you can hardly get cash from Georgia. She and her family have always been most generous, but there are limits, even for the English upper classes.

So the cash, the cash, oh where to get the lolly?

From a Russian energy consortium perhaps. One that wants to deregulate the gas market to allow Russian supplies free access to Western Europe.

The money, the money. The flat, the furniture, Eva. You were even clever with the furniture, avoiding a paper-trail of receipts and Visa statements by buying for cash from trading magazines. Good thinking, but for so much effort you have to be sure she's worth it.

There's the sex. You're nearly forty. For a while, sex hadn't been what it was, not for an oversexed individual like yourself. That's how you think of yourself, isn't it? Proud of the forceful urge, a kind of badge of the profession, proof you belong where the sap always rises. You have drive, energy. You get impassioned, then blocked at every turn. You need outlets. I can understand that.

Eva is sex like it used to be in the beautiful days, way back in Cambridge out on the Backs with Miranda Gadding. Christ yes. The pumping heart, the shimmer. Life did burst then.

Though you express it differently now. With Eva,

in your 'bright red speechless intimacy', you two are apparently 'bridging the gap between man and woman, dissolving.' Needed to write it down, watermarked paper inside a licked envelope, even though she has barely enough English to understand. The letters were a way of writing to yourself. A mistake, Simon. Not so clever.

But Eva is life, is living, that's how you see it, don't you? She protects you from the fear that one year might become much like the next, impossible to remember for itself. An adolescent terror, I think you'll admit, but no less compelling for that. Eva is worth it because she keeps life new, and if life is new, you must be young. That's the sequence, the logic behind the love story, am I right?

Continuing in secret, however, is to live every day with the risk of disclosure, leading to disgrace and certain downfall. Is this then the right option for London MEP Simon Vindolanda? Let me, just for a moment, play devil's advocate.

Why keep the situation as it is when neither your marriage nor your mistress is perfect? I have recorded five separate occasions on which you've joked to political contacts that yours was an arranged marriage. Georgia arranged it. Down to the last detail. But as the details included a marquee and 400 guests and champagne on the lawn of her parents' house near Romsey in Hampshire, it was an arrangement you decided you could live with.

And even though you'd prefer life to be bursting, Eva isn't perfect either. On her trips to Brussels for 'shopping', whenever you snatch twenty minutes to-gether in the Hotel du Congrès, room number 319 (16 minutes 23 seconds the shortest we've put on file), you go in fear for your professional life. When you're in there you rarely talk. Eva's English is not strong, except for the very basic grammar she's learnt by heart, the dog-English you've taught her, a doggerel of love. How does it go?

Love you, you say.

Love you more, she says.

Love you most, you say.

Sweet. Quick. That's your regular shtick, isn't it? Love you most but have to dash. Check your flies, peck on the cheek, check your flies, dash. It can be so miserable.

When you were first elected, representing half a million Londoners, of whom perhaps 200 know you by name, you felt so self-important that you wandered the Euro corridors determined not to fall in love with any girl from Europe who said hello. You did well. Not bad at all after ten years of marriage and out of the house among attractive European women who wear stockings. Though you never picked up the knack of not looking, did you? Can never keep your eyes from flicking down, especially from behind when you think no one's watching. Usually someone is, Simon. It was five years of politics before Eva came along, and by then you were so disillusioned she didn't even have to speak, just sit behind the Russian trade envoy, shuffle a few papers, cross her legs, occasionally make eyes at you above her low-cut square-framed glasses.

At the beginning it was so simple, a perk on Parliament expenses. Dinner-cruises on the Rhine, long drives through northern France with stop-offs for VIP tours of the cellars in Champagne. Eva loved it. You shrugged. That's the kind of guy I am.

In return she went to bed with you, barely out of her teens. You like her to shower first so you can smell her in the flesh, comforting and young like warm plastic beakers. Is that what really gets you going? Is that what set you off the time against a tree in the Orangerie gardens when you came immediately and laughed and said: 'At least it's not raining. Ha ha.'

It started raining. Remember? You wrapped her in your arms, inside your fawn-coloured raincoat, the collar up over her little head as the two of you ran for cover. Hard to keep secrets these days.

But let's not go back, even though the problem with Eva is that it was always perfect yesterday, because you made it through yesterday without being found out. Today is always a risk, and therefore much less enjoyable until it's safely over. And a baby as well. That's going to be tough, nothing but trouble. Trouble doubled.

Which makes #2 Continued Deception hard to recommend, in your case, as a dependable measure for avoiding disgrace. How long can you keep up this charade? Your landscape of danger is increasing, but how much pleasure do you get from stratagems and survival, from travelling everywhere with cash money, a concealed mobile phone and toothbrush? Is that how you want to live, how to get where you want to go? When you first met Eva you were so confident you'd soon have a seat in the House you promised to set her up in London near Madame Tussaud's. It was the only landmark she knew, and she was thrilled. You were so sure, in the good old days.

If your secret life is exposed, it's back to #1 and the drawing board. If you want to avoid the public risk of Denial, and you instinctively understand that in the long run Continued Deception is unsustainable, you might like to consider some further measures we've explored in some detail on your behalf.

3. Reparation/Making Amends

This may be painful. It is not by any means the easy option. You would have to make a decision.

Decide what is the right thing to do, and then do it.

If it is right to stay married to Georgia, and to bring up your children in a stable loving home, then this is a chance to get things right. Before anyone finds out. If you act quickly. And if they do find out, the damage can be minimised by this demonstration of good faith. Voluntarily, under no pressure at all, you'd already decided to do the decent thing.

You do love your wife, you sometimes think. It's so inconvenient to see her unhappy. Georgia is a kind of habit, an attraction easily renewed because you've always loved your English posh. The haughty but naughty, the kind of crisp excitable girls you first met off the meat wagons that came to your boys' school on dance nights. The private boarding school your mum ruined her health to pay for. Then at Cambridge you couldn't resist those fine-grained voices, every rounded vowel a childhood of fresh fruit and Malvern water. The voices you adored, and also the weekends away at houses with tennis courts.

Your girlfriends before Georgia were bumpy and blonde. Georgia was dark though well-built, serious, nice face but thick ankles, not a trophy. She believed that all people were born equal, as had her grandfather, the Minister of Munitions, whose portraits lined the stairs of the family home. You looked at them closely just once, the first time you faced her parents' dismay and were given your own room. Each night you lay there quite happily alone (after some giggly relief from Georgia in one of the bathrooms), listening to the ancient house and loving the sheets, so stiff and clean.

This is what your Mum and Dad had scrimped for, sold all those ice-creams for, to put you in a 'drawing-room' with a girl like Georgia, who you'd met at the University of Cambridge and who, between gin and tonics and dinner, was impossible not to love. Your Mum said she just wanted you to be happy, but you followed your Dad's script and for him it was a weepy: the heights you might one day reach routinely trembled his lip. Georgia was duly written in and you wouldn't want to give her up now, nor the town-house in Pimlico, or the cottage near Marlborough, wouldn't want to make Dad cry again. He cries easily, your Dad.

It's not too late. Don't be a bastard husband all your life, thinking a happy marriage means she's reliable at social events. Remember what's good about Georgia, and why you loved her in the first place. You could make her laugh, remember, and enflame her with your socialist principles; being young and poor you had to use your personality. No VIP trips, no expenses, that's not the kind of guy you were.

Or if not in the first place, later when she was pregnant. You were surprised by how beautiful she became, and you held her hand more tightly than you should, more tightly than you had before. Oh the fun before Hugh was born, remember that? The two of you keeping the anxiety at bay by larking around, and in the last days before birth saying 'fuck' as often as possible. Fuck this, fuck that, her in her high crystal tones, Lawdy! These fucking false contractions can fuck the fuck off! As much swearing as possible, while you still could, before the baby came and you were on your best behaviour, supposedly for the rest of your lives.

Hugh Walter Vindolanda, soon followed by Madeleine Federica Vindolanda. For the first time in your life you had something of your own to lose. Think of that now, of the kids, those poor privileged children. You have to work at marriage, make it a long-life proposition. Throw in some additives, some colouring, some white lies and foreign holidays, and accept it for what it is: a processed, preserved love, less tasty maybe but also less perishable.

This is the way back for you, Simon. Do the right thing, stop seeing Eva, and then look forward to years of buying back your soul. This will be your penance, and it will do you good. I mean it. You've acted badly. Now find out if there's a way back to the better person you were. Be ambitious closer to home, work at a future for you and Georgia and the children. Vow to make things right and act your age, for the years will become indistinguishable. That's how you will survive with Georgia. She will block the light, she will provide shade. What more do you want?

Eva.

Forget Eva. Enjoy the postponed approval of Georgia's parents, of your Dad, of your dear departed Mum (god rest her soul). Be pragmatic. Divorce is unthinkable, not because of the children but the grandparents. Enjoy what marriage has brought you, and pity those poor fools who married for love. Looking back, wondering how it happened, they must feel very embarrassed if love was the one good reason.

Besides, it was Georgia's cousin the Right Honourable Member for Andover who first mooted that safe Westminster seat. Between men, keeping it in the family, he offered you a word to the wise:

'You do understand, Simon, if you have any muck they will find it. Clean out the stables, old boy.'

As for Eva, you need to deconjugate your flimsy little grammar of love. Agreeable though she may have been, regrettable though it is to break such shattering news, Eva has been a fling. Making her, at this critical stage of coping with potential disgrace, the something flung.

Face facts: you've wilfully ignored her past, even though you know that no one comes all new. You have the basics. She's 23, dress-size 6, shoe-size 4. But you don't want to uncover more awkward truths it's difficult to shop for. A perky little number like Eva. In a studio flat so ideal for the European Institutions. In a town you only visit seriously four days in every month. Is it likely that you're the one and only candidate for father of Eva's child?

Forgive me. You've often thought of giving Eva up and going back to your wife. Most men in your position do, and wish the process were easier. Unfortunately,

Eva may not go quietly. It might take cash you don't have. You like Eva. You live for those twenty minutes at a times. And so, unable to make a decision, you hum and you ha. You shilly and shally and before you can do the right thing someone finds you out. Funny that. And then you're thrown back on #1, Denial.

As I think I've already mentioned, no one's going to believe you.

4. Confession/Confrontation

More modern, even radical. Confront the situation. Confess right left and centre. You have a family you love and a mistress you need. Tell the world and your wife that this is the way it is and the way you want it to stay. We can work it out. All you need is love. It's the twenty-first century.

A tricky measure to pull off, this one, but if it's truly what you want, truly, truly, you might find the courage to give it a try. Why be ashamed? Where the disgrace? Go back to Georgia and live a full life with Eva. If you're man enough then this is the bold, honest approach. And there's no disgrace in that.

Honesty will put a lump in your throat, and it may bring a tear to your eye. But remember what your boarding school education taught you from such an early age (eight! Sent away from home at eight years old!). If it doesn't feel tough and tearful, like going back to school, it isn't life at all. It's just the holidays.

You can do this, a man like you. The wife and mistress muddle is commonplace for a very good reason. Social expectations are outdated and at fault. Individuals of energy and drive need more than one lover, and politicians of our European partner nations fully understand this. We should make an effort to integrate and to understand it too. There is no dishonour! No need for reproach. It's only natural.

You are highly sexed (always have been), you are driven, you have needs. Explain this gently to Georgia.

You love your loyal wife and you love your little children. Explain this to Eva.

Proactive and honest, you may well be applauded for your openness and your ability to control events. You have the sap rising, no question (23 years old!), but you are also responsible and transparent. The way you have managed your affairs is original and refreshing, in this day and age plain and morally right, and such an audacious step could be the making of a maverick and his limitless political destiny. The biographers will eat this up. Twice the man, you managed a pair of families, brought stability to a federacy of nations.

You should, however, exercise caution. If you choose this means of coping, neither #1 Denial or #2 Continued Deception will ever be feasible again. You have to be certain that this wife and this mistress are the ones with whom you'll make your stand.

Eva is special, you sometimes think. She can make you hate yourself for the time you wasted before you knew her. That's a good start, and the thrill of the Strasbourg apartment is yet to fade. In session, always in the afternoon while the Spanish delegates sleep, you let the Venetian blind drop and block out the river, and every time it falls it makes a sound as hopeful and exciting as a fishing reel. With Eva, as you turn your back to the black and blinded window, you never know what you're going to get, though you always get something.

It's such a relief, isn't it, such a change? All that talking in the vast Parliament chamber, to get almost nothing done. Then the tiny spaces of the flat and the not talking, and getting everything done.

Frankly, in my considered opinion, owning up honestly to your needs has a better chance of success than #3 Making Amends. Doing the right thing under duress, like a duty, is a kind of imprisonment, as if perhaps it wasn't the right thing to do after all. Think of it. London and Georgia, and finding conversation for the next twenty years to use up time before you die. How does it go? In the drawing room with her parents, or over cocktails with friends; the uses of homeopathy, or astronomy, the legitimacy of fish-knives or Scottish tartans. House prices.

Keep Georgia, but keep Eva too. Nurture that vague, vain idea of love as peace and charity, as constant forgiveness. Give it a chance and it might come true.

If this seems far-fetched, think back to how far-fetched marriage once seemed, before you were actually married. Remember how hard and shiny were the white-gold wedding bands when you got them back from the jewellers. You tried them both on, and yours felt loose on your finger. It had room to grow into, as if the South Kensington jeweller assumed marriage must automatically make a man plumper, more conceited. Hers, on your little finger, felt a little tight as you wandered blinged up in your underpants around your best man's flat, but then it wasn't designed for you to wear.

Georgia might come round to this new arrangement, like she did to dirty nappies and sleepless nights and the fit of her wedding ring. You've both adapted before now — no more swearing, long periods apart, waiting for Westminster. Adapt again.

If she screams at you when you suggest this measure, attacks you physically or reacts in any other violent or extreme manner, all to the good. Rage and fury prove your relationship is still alive, so think of this as a ripple in the expanse of a golden fifty-year marriage. A storm in a tea-cup. Though do remember, while it rages, to pretend that the storm is more important than the cup.

No? Not for you? Even after seven years in the parliament you don't feel sufficiently European. You don't see this as a measure that's likely to work. Not face to face, man to mistress, husband to wife. You're not bold or honest enough. If you were, you wouldn't so often be in touch with your blackmailers.

Which effectively rules out #4 Confession/ Confrontation. Fair enough. Your call. It was always a long shot, but you mustn't forget that doing nothing is not for you an option.

5. Blame Someone Else

It will come to light eventually, even if:

1.   You haven't denied it
2.   You've tried to hide it
3.   You haven't corrected it
4.   You were unable to confront it

Georgia will find out, and the party machine will find out, and your Dad and your in-laws and your children will find out. Why? Because Eva, and the people it now seems she works for, are threatening to reveal the full story with intimate details and photographs.

It's the secrecy that makes you vulnerable. Whether you like it or not, you've become the balancing act in a standard conditional sentence:

'If you do not . . ., we will . . .'

And each time you do, they always seem to find something new and ungainly to fill the fresh and empty pan on your sorry side of the scales. On theirs, the weight remains always the same.

Or we will expose your affair with Eva Kuznetsova.

If you do not lobby for an amendment to the bill on gas deregulation.

If you do not vote against anti-corruption clause 3f (Business and Gift Addendum).

If you do not introduce visiting businessman Sergei A to visiting minister Sir Adrian B.

If you do not, within the next twenty-four hours, acquire three family passes to EuroDisney for a specific date in December.

If you do not.

We will expose your affair with Eva Kuznetsova, and also the fact that she's carrying your child.

You have gone along with this for a while, but the demands will get bigger, or smaller. Either way, disgrace looms. You have to come clean, find a way of coping with the situation, escape with some integrity and a shot at the future intact.

Blame other people.

Try and lever some sympathy: you are trapped among vipers. Oh yes you are.

Georgia, for a start. What was she thinking of, dividing her time between London and Brussels when you were so often in Strasbourg? She should have kept a closer eye on you, stifled your fantasies at birth, including, most unkindly, your fantasy of happiness with another woman. You and Georgia still have sex, we know that, but she's impossible to trust, especially when she wriggles and moans. The signals say she's having a good time, but as she has her eyes closed and her head ricked back she can't see you looking her over and wondering. Not whether she's faking. You know she is. But is she faking it because she wants you to be happy, or because she wants to hurry you up?

No wonder you looked elsewhere, and Eva used sex to trap you, a lonely public servant far from home suffering for a tottering continent. And what gratitude did you get for that? Blame the European parliament and the European people. You wouldn't have got into this mess in London, not if you were a regular British MP at Westminster, because this kind of thing has become unworkable. The tabloids, the public relations; at least back home someone cares.

Georgia's parents. They knew you weren't the right kind of husband for their daughter, and her father would often say so. Way outside the acceptable gene pool. By capitulating, just because it was what Georgia wanted, they also gave you the contacts and confidence to follow up in politics. And now stop and look at the car crash. Feel the strain and the stress. It's very fashionable these days, is stress, very excusable, very usable. Now that I think of it, you could bring up some previous, like the time after the sock incident when Georgia suggested you see a psychiatrist.

'I know what we'd talk about,' you said.

She should have forced the issue. It was her conjugal duty. Instead, she trod softly: 'So why don't you go?'

'Don't want to talk about it.'

It was your parents' fault, who never showed you enough affection. Your Mum died, quite selfishly really, and Dad was only interested in social mobility, keeping you on course at boarding school where you started at the age of eight. Eight years old! You met some of the better people and were very cold at night and received a thoroughly English education, with the live-in teachers never in danger of anthropomorphising the children. You took on board the absence of love and the rules of cricket, which require a firm grasp of what cricket is not.

You discovered a talent for what cricket is not. This, and the fact that your parents sold ice-creams, led to variable self esteem. You needed to prove yourself, and you're now facing disgrace.

At a stretch, this is also Hugh and Madeleine's fault. Let's not leave anyone out. Kids are so demanding. At the beginning, they stopped you from doing what you wanted. Now, they give Georgia an excuse for not wanting to do anything at all. Stuck, going nowhere, terrified of the same old shoeshine, you took unilateral action. Under the circumstances, who could possibly blame you?

6. Running Away

Otherwise known as resigning your elected post to spend more time with your family. This can be combined with #3 Making Amends, but the two measures are often unconnected.

It will be apparent to you that our measures to cope with disgraceful and other events are becoming more extreme. Alas, so is your predicament. Eva's people have decided that you may be of more use to them in London, especially if you agitate for a junior ministerial position in the Department of Trade and Industry. I believe this is where your good friend Georgia's cousin works. It is early days, but it seems we all know you're about to be offered the safe constituency of Sheffield West. You are being encouraged and congratulated on all sides. This means more people than ever stand to be disappointed, or so is the opinion of that nice young woman from MI6 who phoned to invite you to tea. She said her name was Higgins.

Before your life gets totally out of hand, why not postpone just about everything?

Go back to London, live off Georgia's trust-fund, spend more time with the children. Everyone seems to agree that success is poison, so why the big rush? Disappear, take a break. It doesn't have to be with the family, because whoever you end up with, the time comes when you see how selfish they are, in the sense that they're not always thinking about you, just as you're not thinking about them.

Of course not. You're thinking about yourself.

Take this one last chance, alone and free, to find out who you are. Go to the seaside. You love the seaside. Stay in a guest-house and study the waves. Walk along the shore and build sandcastles, because it's never too late to have a happy childhood. Play some of that golf you've been pretending to play.

Life outside the spotlight could be better than you've ever dared expect. Somewhere in the English provinces you could reinvent yourself, forgetting your ancestors and your second-generation Dad. Be no one's son or father or husband or lover, but whoever you alone want to be. It can be done.

It doesn't have to be beside the seaside. You could blot yourself into some sunny corner of Europe where the wine trees grow. Live wherever the foreign language makes you an idiot, where you understand nothing and squeeze the nearest tube and put hair-gel on your toothbrush. Regress, stop, start again. Choose another life, another career. Off the top of your head: wood-turner.

Turn wood and drink wine and wait. Will there be sex? Like asking will there be sky. Romantic love that surges and ring-a-ding-dings, outside in summer-time and skirts, ripe and obvious like silver trumpets. You will simply cease to subscribe to the doctrines of effort and repentance. You will kick back. Disgrace will have no dominion.

Untroubled, a craggy old rogue, you'll evolve into a close enough copy of your grandfather. You'll spend a great deal of time in a garage with the door swung up, safe among the smell of onions and garlic drying on hooks. You too will have your rows of oiled tools on hooks on the walls, and creped stacks of chamois leathers, and days of grace slowly told and gravy for lunch. Remember what he used to say?

We are all very small, Simon, and time goes by. So calm down.

That's what he used to say. I know that because you passed it on as pillow-talk to Eva, who I don't believe was listening.

If you run away, Georgia will be fine. Her sense of family doesn't always include you as it is. And once the kids move up and she's on the school run, she'll probably meet a dozen suitable husbands every weekday morning. Private school, of course. Like yours. Only better.

Her parents will pay. No need to think twice. Look at your finger, man, you never did grow into that wedding ring. Marriage never set free that fat contented fellow the jeweller imagined inside you. Nobody knows who you are, not really. So go ahead and escape while you still can. Run away. Run.

Now. Alone. Where. How much stuff to take and

who to tell and what about money. Is this temporary or long term?

It's a cry for help, Simon.

But you can't run away, not you. You know in your bones that politics is all life and your career is a very real treasure in times of need. The sun orbits Westminster. If you run, you're finished, as surely as if you issue a denial. They will assume disgrace, even if they don't have the facts. They may not even bother to find you.

7. Suicide

A man of honour, a true English gentleman, might have come to this conclusion sooner. The pills and the booze, the blade in the bath. No place to be weak, Simon, no place to be weak.

You wonder how strong you are. Better to deal in certainties, and it's quite certain you never became the man you were meaning to become. Can't argue with that. Feel sorry for yourself, get angry. Be astonished by your own superficiality, how poorly you've lived, how little you've cared for the light and the truth. A part of you, still fighting on, protests you left no stone unturned, hence young Eva. You wanted to know if there was something better, and then when the blackmail cut in you weren't sure it was any worse pretending that Europe needed Russian gas than pretending the European Parliament was just the place for an ambitious young politico like you. Working for money, marrying for money, helping one country, helping another, the lines all blurred.

Most of them, Simon, not all. You were always on the same track, interested in nothing much except your own esteem, the comfort of your inflated sense of self. In your quest for the meaning of life, at which you only get the one go, you have indeed left no stone unturned. Ha. Except for any of the heavy ones.

You disgust yourself. You have nowhere left to turn.

The blade in the bath and then you're done. No more falling on your feet. No more falling.

The trouble with suicide is that it gives so much value to life. If you conclude that life is so utterly pointless that it's not worth living, then life is not really worth not living, either. Makes little difference either way.

I don't see you as a suicide, not you, Simon. You couldn't do it. Not to yourself.

8. Murder

This idea came from the unemotional, almost inhuman mind of Miss Higgins, or so one day you will allow yourself to believe.

But it's also true that you get bored with the idea

of disgrace, both its inevitability and how mundane it seems. The hidden mistress is such a tawdry and common way to fail.

Higgins sips her tea, puts the cup delicately back in the saucer, shrugs. Higgins says no Eva equals no problems with your wife. The Russians who have been such close friends to Eva think the same thing, now they want you in London. As it happens, Higgins too wants the Russians to want you in London. She suggests, in your nearest café Le Roi et Son Fou, while dissecting a blood-red linzertorte with a cake fork, that you could be of assistance by reporting back on what the Russians want from you (three family passes to Legoland and the projected subsidies for nuclear fuel).

Or we will expose your affair with Eva Kuznetsova

Who will? They will. We will. Holy Moses. Everyone will.

To accept the kind of arrangement offered by young Miss Higgins is surely an elegant way for Euro MP and future parliamentary high-flyer Simon Vindolanda to avoid disgrace. Your ruination simply won't be allowed to happen, or not now, not yet. You will be looked after and cared for, just as you have been shepherded for some time now without your knowledge. We have been listening and watching. You are now being offered the unusual opportunity to submit to higher forces who understand you because they know you, we know everything there is to know about you. Such is life, under Her Majesty's wing.

Unfortunately, in this scheme of things, Eva has to go. Higgins is not an impulsive character, but was perhaps ahead of you when she politely suggested that Eva is in a very dangerous profession.

'What?' You pretended not to hear or understand her, I rather think the latter. 'Former assistant to the Russian trade envoy at the Strasbourg European Parliament?'

'Whore,' Higgins said.

Don't feign such shock. We're much alike, you, me, young Miss Higgins. We all like to think things through to the deadest end, and on this occasion here is where the thinking leads. Higgins showed you the photographs of Eva in leather leaning against a crash barrier on the underpass beneath the A49 to Colmar. That was before she met you. It isn't difficult for the Russians to find recruits in this part of the world. At the underpass, waiting for the German-plated cars, nearly all the girls are Russian.

Higgins will have told you we don't actually have to act. In fact we should do nothing, except wait and watch. The Russians will take care of Eva in their own time, in their own way, but you weren't happy with that, were you, Simon? Not happy at all. Even if the Russians are careful with Eva, late at night in the cold-flowing river, drunk on vodka I should think, poor lost and careless lass, then you'll still know what really happened. So will Higgins. We'll all be accomplices to murder. Which is true, and don't forget the Russians will know that you know. Probably make sure of it, more weight on their side of the blackmail balance. And although Higgins also knows, the Russians don't know about Higgins.

Exciting, isn't it? No two years will ever be the same again.

Leave Brussels and Strasbourg behind. Move on to Westminster where you always wanted to be, no one the wiser. That's what Higgins said. Exact words, and we can play them back to you as many times as we like, as so much else.

'I won't do it.'

'What is more disgraceful?' That's Higgins again, using her sensible tea-time voice, 'this, a chance to help your country, or the inevitability of failing at your job and sinking into obscurity as a disgraced Euro MP? Not even a very memorable scandal, to tell the truth.'

You'll get tired of Eva, you know. Name of the game. It's hard, and for your own peace of mind I appreciate that you'd prefer to tire of other people before they tire of you. Nothing's perfect. But in our line of work Evas come and go, and I have a feeling you're going to last at this. You have an eventful career ahead of you. You've already proved yourself adept at the hole-in-the-wallery, so why not the cloak-and-the-daggery?

I wouldn't want Higgins to have to withdraw her offers of protection and assistance. The Russians won't be very happy with you. They'll call in the balance of the conditional. A few well-placed rumours. You and Eva. The imminent happy event. Then what?

'I won't stand by while somebody gets killed!'

Your voice became quite high-pitched at this point, despite the nobility of the sentiment. From the video footage I can see in your eyes that you believe it, for the time being.

'For Christ sake she's pregnant. Have some heart.'

'Is alleged to be pregnant,' Higgins corrected you. Then she left, without deadlines or ultimatums. She did not leave her details. Even her, Simon, even Higgins, you watched her closely as she walked away. Just as we were watching you.

We can see it in your eyes, Simon. You're not ready to take advice. Not yet, not on this cycle.

But what else can you possibly do?

1. Denial

As you stand up in front of the microphones and cameras you'll have a lump like uncooked pastry in your throat. It will feel bad, wrong, horribly self-destructive. It will feel like going back to school, like real life.

Reading from a prepared statement, you will say that you simply do not accept the unfounded and malicious allegations that have been made against you. You have no idea why or how they originated. You have never been in contact with any inappropriate individuals or organisations and wish only to continue with your life as a family man and an active member of the European Parliament. You trust that from now on you and your family will be left alone.

No one believes it, not even you.

2. Concealment/Continued Deception

Come on, Simon, jump ahead. We both know where this is going.

The People on Privilege Hill
Jane Gardam

DRENCHING, SOAKING, RELENTLESS rain. Black cold rain for
black cold winter Dorsetshire. Edward Feathers loved
rain but warm rain, falling through oriental air, steam
rising from sweating earth, dripping, glistening drops
that rolled across banana leaves, rain that wetted the
pelts of monkeys. Bloody Dorset, his retirement home.
He was cold and old. He was cold and old and going out
to lunch with a woman called Dulcie he'd never much
liked. His wife Betty had been dead some years.

'I am rich,' announced Feathers – Sir Edward Feathers QC – to his affluent surroundings. On the walls of
the vestibule of his house hung watercolours of Ben-
gal and Malaya painted a hundred years ago by English
memsahibs under parasols, sitting at their easels out of
doors in long petticoats and cotton skirts with tulle and
ribbons and painting aprons made of something called
'crash'.

Very good, too, those paintings, he thought. Worth a lot of money now.

Under his button-booted feet was a rug from Tashkent. Nearby stood a throne of rose-coloured silk, very tattered. Betty had fallen in love with it once, in Dacca. Nearby was a brass and ironwood umbrella stand with many spikes sticking out of it. Feathers turned to the umbrella stand, chose an umbrella, shook it loose: a fine black silk with a malacca handle and initialled gold band. He did not open it in the house on account of the bad luck this would unleash. A fresh wave of rain lashed at the windows. 'I could order a cab,' he said aloud. He had been a famous barrister and the sound of his voice had been part of his fortune. The old 'Oxford accent', now very rare, comforted him sometimes. 'I am rich. It's only a few minutes away. The fare is not the issue. It is a matter of legs. If I lose the use of my legs,' he said, for he was far into his eighties, 'I'm finished. I shall walk.'

Rain beat against the fanlight above the front door. There was a long ring on the bell and a battering at the knocker. His neighbour stood there in a dreadful anorak and without an umbrella.

'Oh yes, Veneering,' said Feathers, unenthusiastic. 'You'd better come in. But I'm just going out.'

'May I share your car?' asked Veneering. 'To Dulcie's?'

'I'm not taking the car.' (Veneering was the

meanest man ever to make a fortune at the Bar except for old what's-his-name, Fiscal-Smith, in the north.) 'By the time I've got it out of the garage and turned it round I could be there. I didn't know you were going to Dulcie's.'

'Oh yes. Big do,' said Veneering. 'Party for some cousin. We 'll walk together, then. Are you ready?'

Feathers was wearing a magnificent twenty-year-old double-breasted three-piece suit. All his working life he had been called Filth not only because of the old joke (Failed In London Try Hong Kong) but because nobody had ever seen him other than immaculate: scrubbed, polished, barbered, manicured, brushed, combed, per-fect. At any moment of his life Feathers could have been presented to the Queen.

'Are *you* ready?' he asked.

'I'll take the anorak off ', said Veneering, his scruffy old rival who now lived next door, 'when we get there. Don't *you* need a coat?'

'I have my umbrella,' said Feathers.

'Oh yes, I could borrow one of your umbrellas. Thanks.' And Veneering stepped in from the downpour bringing some of it with him. He squelched over to the Benares pillar and started poking about, coming up with a delicate pink parasol with a black tassel.

Both men regarded it.

'No,' said Feathers. 'That's a lady's parasol. Betty's.'

Veneering ran his arthritic fingers down the silk.

Outside the rain had hushed. 'Just for down the road,' he said. 'I'd enjoy carrying it. I remember it.'

'It's not on offer,' said Feathers. 'Sorry.'

But Veneering, like some evil gnome, was over the doorstep again, introducing the parasol to the outer air. It flew up at once, giving a glow to his face as he looked up into its lacquered struts. He twirled it about. 'Aha,' he said.

Down came the rain again and Feathers, with a leo-nine roar of disgust, turned back to the umbrella-stand. Somewhere in the bottom of it were stubby common umbrellas that snapped open when you pressed a but-ton. Right for Veneering.

'We 'll be late,' said Veneering from the drive, considering Feathers's old man's backside bent over the umbrella-stand, floppy down the backs of his thighs. (Losing his flanks. Bad sign. Senile.) Veneering still had the bright blue eyes of a young man. Cunning eyes. And strong flanks. 'In fact we're late already. It's after one.' He knew that to be late was for Feathers a mortal sin.

So Feathers abandoned the search, checked his pockets for house keys, slammed the front door behind him and sprang off down the drive on his emu legs under an impeccable blackdome, overtaking Veneer-ing's short but sturdy legs, that thirty years ago had bestridden the colony of Hong Kong and the interna-tional legal world — and quite a few of its women.

Veneering trotted, under the apricot satin, way behind.

One behind the other they advanced up the village hill beneath overhanging trees, turned to the right by the church, splashed on. It was rather further to walk than Feathers had remembered. On they went in silence except for the now only murmuring rain, towards Privilege Road.

Dulcie's address was Privilege House, seat at one time, she said, of the famous house of the Privé-Lièges who had arrived with the Conqueror. Those who had lived in the village all their lives – few enough now – were doubtful about the Privé-Lièges and thought that as children they had been told of some village privies once constructed up there. Dulcie's husband, now dead, had said, 'Well, as long as nobody tells Dulcie. Unless of course the privies were Roman.' He had been a lawyer too and had retired early to the south-west to read Thomas Hardy. He'd had private means, and needed them with Dulcie.

There had been some Hardy-esque dwellings around Privilege House with thatch and rats, but now these were glorified as second homes with gloss paint and lined curtains and polished door knockers. The owners came thundering down now and then on Friday nights in cars like Iraqi tanks stuffed with food from suburban farmers' markets. They thundered back to London on the Monday morning. Gravel and laurel had appeared around the cottages and in front of Dulcie's Norman demesne. A metal post said 'Privilege Road'. The post had distressed her. But she was an unbeatable woman.

Feathers paused at the top of the hill outside a cot (four bed, two bath) and called over his shoulder, 'Who the hell is this?' For a squat sort of fellow was approaching from a lateral direction, on their port bow. He presented himself into the rain as a pair of feet and an umbrella spread over the body at waist level. Head down, most of him was invisible. The umbrella had spikes sticking out here and there, and the cloth was tattered and rusty. A weapon that had known campaigns.

When it came up close, the feet stopped and the umbrella was raised to reveal a face as hard as wood.

'Good God!' said Veneering. 'It's Fiscal-Smith,' and the rain began to bucket down again upon the three of them.

'Oh, good morning,' said Fiscal-Smith. 'Haven't seen you, Feathers, since just after Betty died. Haven't seen you, Veneering, since that embarrassing little matter in the New Territories. Nice little case. Nice little milch cow for me. Pity the way they went after you in the Law Reports. Are you going to Dulcie 's?'

'I suppose you're the cousin,' said Veneering.
'What cousin? I was a friend of poor old Bill till he dropped me for Thomas Hardy. Come on, let's keep goingI'm getting wet.'

In single file the three old judges pressed ahead: black silk, apricot toile and bundle of prongs.

Fiscal-Smith made uncouth noises that in another man might have indicated mirth, and they reached Dulcie 's tall main gate, firmly closed. Through the wrought iron there was very much on view a lawn and terrace of simulated stone and along the side of the house a conservatory that was filled with coloured moons. They were umbrellas all open and all wet.

'Whoever can be coming?' said Feathers, who originally had thought he was the only guest. 'Must be dozens.'

'Yes, there was some point to the cousin,' said Veneering, 'but I can't remember what. She talks too fast.'

'It's a monk,' said Fiscal-Smith. 'Not a cousin but a monk. Though of course a monk *could* be a cousin. Look at John the Baptist.'

'A monk? At Dulcie's?'

'Yes. A Jesuit. He 's off to the islands to prepare for his final vows. This is his last blow-out. She's taking him to the airport afterwards, as soon as we 've left.'

Feathers winced at 'blow-out'. He was not a Catholic, or anything, really, except when reading the Book of Common Prayer or during the Sunday C of E service if it was 1666, but he didn't like to hear of a 'blow-out' before vows.

'*What* airport?' asked Veneering. 'Our airport? The airport at the end of the universe?' for he sometimes read modern books.

Feathers, who did not, suspected nastiness.

'Dulcie 's a kind woman,' he said, suppressing the slight thrill of excitement at the thought of her puffy raspberry lips. 'Very kind. And the wine will be good. But she 's obviously asked a horde,' he added with a breath of regret. 'There are dozens of umbrellas.'

In the conservatory trench six or so of them seemed to stir, rubbing shoulders like impounded cattle.

Feathers, the one who saw Dulcie most often, knew that the wrought-iron gate was never unlocked and was only a viewing station, so he led the way round the house and they were about to left-wheel into a gravel patch when a car – ample but not urban – pounced up behind them, swerved in front of them, swung round at the side door and blocked their path. Doors were flung open and a lean girl with a cigarette in her mouth jumped out. She ground the cigarette stub under her heel, like the serpent in Eden, and began to decant two disabled elderly women. They were supplied with umbrellas and directed, limping, to the door. One of them had a fruity cough. The three widowed judges might have been spectres.

'God!' said Fiscal-Smith. 'Who are they?'

'It's the heavenly twins,' said Feathers with one of

his roaring cries. 'Sing in the church choir. Splendidly.'
He found himself again defensive about the unloved
territory of his old age and surprised himself. When
had Fiscal-Smith last been near a church? Or bloody
Veneering? Never.

'Who's the third?' asked Fiscal-Smith. 'Is she local?'

'She 'll be the carer,' said Feathers. 'Probably from
Lithuania.'

'This is going to be a rave,' said Veneering, and
Feathers felt displeased again and almost said, 'We 're
all going to get old *one* day,' but remembered that he 'd
soon be ninety.

A blaze of yellow light washed suddenly across the
rainy sky, ripping the clouds and silhouetting the tree
clumps on Privilege Hill. He thought: I should have
brought something for Dulcie, some flowers. Betty
would have brought flowers. Or jam or something. And
was mortified to see some sort of offering emerging
from Veneering's disgusting anorak and – great heav-
en! – something appearing in Fiscal-Smith's mean paw.
Feathers belonged to an age when you didn't take pres-
ents or write thank-you letters for luncheon but he
wasn't sure, all at once, that Dulcie did. He glared at
Fiscal-Smith's rather old-looking package.

'It's a box of tea,' said Fiscal-Smith. 'Christmas-pud-
ding flavour from Fortnum and Mason. I've had it for
years. I'm not sure if you can get it now. Given it by a
client before I took Silk. In the sixties.'

'I wonder what the monk will bring,' said Veneering. He seemed to be cheering up, having seen the carer's legs.

And here was Dulcie coming to welcome them, shrieking prettily in grey mohair and pearls; leading them to the pool of drying umbrellas. 'Just drop them down. In the conservatory trough. It's near the hot pipes. It's where I dry my dahlias. They love it. Don't they look pretty? Sometimes I think they'll all rise into the air.'

(She's insane, thought Feathers.)

'And I must run to my soufflé,' she called. 'Do go in. Get a drink. Awful rain. So good of you to come out. Introduce yourselves.'

In the sitting room there was no sign of the guest of honour. The carer was pouring herself an enormous drink. The cleaning lady of the village, Kate, was handing round titbits. She knew the guests intimately. 'I told you not to wear that shirt until I'd turned the collar,' she hissed at Veneering.

They all drank and the rain rattled down on the glass roof of the umbrella house. The clocks ticked.

'What's that over there?' asked Veneering.

A boy was regarding them from a doorway.

'A boy, I think,' said Feathers, a childless man.

'Maybe this is the cousin. Hello there! Who're you? Are you Dulcie's young cousin?'

The boy said nothing but padded after them as

they carried their drinks into another room, where he continued to stare. 'Hand the nuts round,' said Kate the cleaner. 'Be polite,' but the boy took no notice. He approached Veneering and inspected him further.

'Why ever should I be Granny's cousin?'

Veneering, unused for many years to being cross-questioned, said, 'We understood we were to meet a cousin.'

'No. It's a monk. Do you play music?'

'Me?' said Veneering. 'Why?'

'I just wondered. I play cello and drums.'

'Oh. Good!'

'In America. I'm an American citizen. I don't come over often.'

'That explains everything.' (God, I'm hungry!)

'What do you mean?'

'Don't you say "sir" in America? I thought all American children were polite now.'

'Actually, not all. Sir. I know one who goes straight over to the fridge in people 's houses and looks in to see what they've got.'

(Fiendishly hungry.)

'Would you have guessed I was American? I don't do the voice. I *can* do the voice but only at school. My parents are British. I won't salute the flag either.'

'You have a lot of confidence. How old are you?'

'I'm eight. But I'm not confident. I don't do anything wrong. I believe in God. I say my prayers.'

'I think we 're all getting into deep water here,' said Fiscal-Smith, carrying away his gin-and-mixed. 'Off you go, boy. Help in the kitchen.'

The boy took no notice. He was concentrating on Veneering. 'Sir,' he said, 'do you, by any chance, play the drums?'

'*Off* you go now!' cried Dulcie, sweeping in and pushing the child under her grandmotherly arm out of the path of the three great men. 'This is Herman. My grandson. He's eight. I'm giving my daughter a break. Herman, pass the nuts.'

***

'My *wretched* monk,' Dulcie said. 'I don't think we 'll wait. Oh, well, if you're sure you don't mind. The souf-flé will be ready in about ten minutes and then we *can't* wait a *moment* more.' (Feathers's tummy rumbled.)

'But *do* you play the drums?' insisted Herman, cir-cling Veneering before whose face hardened criminals had crumbled. Herman's face held up.

'I do, as a matter of fact,' Veneering said, turning away to take a canapé.

'They've given me some. Granny did. For my birth-day. Come and see.'

And like Mary's lamb, Judge Veneering followed the child to a chaotic playroom where drums in all their glory wereset up near a piano.

'I didn't know there was a piano here,' said Veneering to himself, but aloud. 'And a Bechstein.' He sat down and played a little.

Herman hove up alongside and said, 'You're good. I knew you'd be good.'

'Are you good?'

'No. Not at piano. I do a bit of cello. It's mostly the drums.'

Veneering, feet among toys, began to tap his toes and the Bechstein sang. Then it began to sing more nois- ily and Veneering closed his eyes, put his chin in the air and howled like a dog.

'Hey. Great!' said Herman, thumping him.

'Honky-tonk.' Veneering began to bob up and down.

'What's honky-tonk? D'you want to hear some drumming? Sir?'

'*Herman*,' called his grandmother.

'Better go,' said Veneering. Then he let his voice become a black man's voice and began singing the Blues.

'Better not,' said Herman. 'Well, not before lunch.'

The child sat close against Veneering at the table, gazing up at his yellow old face.

'Herman, pass the bread,' said Dulcie, but all Her- man did was ask, 'Did you ever have a boy like me that played drums?'

'I did,' said Veneering, surprising people.

'After lunch can we have a go at them?'

'Eat your soufflé,' said Dulcie, and Herman obediently polished it off, wondering why something so deflated and leathery should be considered better than doughnuts or cake.

There was a pause after the plates were taken away and, unthinkably, Veneering, his eyes askew with gin and wine, excused himself and made again for the piano, Herman trotting behind.

'Oh no, I won't have this,' said Dulcie.

'America, I suppose,' said Feathers.

A torrent of honky-tonk flowed out of the playroom and some loud cries. The drums began.

Bass drums, floor-tom, normal-tom, cymbals. High-hat, crash-ride, thin *crash!* And now, *now*, the metallic stroking, the brush, the whispering ghost – listen, listen – and now the big bass drum. Hammers on the pedals, cross arms, cross legs, tap tap, paradiddle, paradiddle, *let go*! Hammer on pedal now then – HIGH HAT! CRASH RIDE! THIN CRASH!

The glass doors of the conservatory, now filming up, shook as if they'd received the tremors of a not-too-distant earthquake, and a new sound joined the drums as Veneering began to sing and almost outstrip the tremors. Not a word could be heard round the dining table and Dulcie rushed out of the room. As she left, came the crescendo and the music ceased, to reverberations and cackling laughter.

'*Herman*! Please return to the table. Don't dare to monopolise Judge Veneering.'

And Herman, staggering dazed from the mountain tops, let his small jaw drop and fell off his perch, scattering instruments.

Veneering sat on at the piano, hands on knees, chin on chest, enwrapped in pleasure. Then quietly, he began to play again.

'No – I'm sorry, Terry' – she had remembered his nasty little name – 'I'm sorry but I think the latecomer has just arrived. Come at once.'

There was a commotion going on in the hall.

'Dear Terry – *please*. It's boeuf bourguignon.'

Veneering jumped up and embraced her, grinning. 'Honkytonk!' he said. 'He's good, that boy. Tremendous on the normaltom. Could hear that bass a quarter-mile away. Beautiful brush on the snare.' He went back to the dining room rubbing his hands. 'Been playing the Blues,' he said to one and all.

'You haven't,' said Herman.

'Well, the Pale-Rose Pinks,' said Veneering. 'Near enough.'

'Veneering, more wine,' said Feathers warningly.

'Much better not,' said Fiscal-Smith.

The two damaged sisters sat, making patterns on the damask with their fingers.

'Hey! Could he play as well as me, your son?' asked Herman in an American accent.

There was a pause.

'Probably,' said Veneering.

'Did he make it? Was he a star? In music?'

'No. He died.'

'What did he die of?'

'Be quiet, boy!' Feathers roared.

'Now,' said Dulcie. 'Now, I do believe – here is our monk. Father Ambrose. On his way to St Umbrage 's on the island of Skelt.'

'Bullet,' said Veneering. 'Soldier.'

'It's stupid to be a soldier if you can play music.'

'As you say. Quite so. Now, get on with your lunch, boy. We 've plainsong ahead of us.'

But the plainsong was not to be. Nor did the monk join them for lunch. Kate the cleaner put her head round the diningroom door and asked to speak to Dulcie for a moment – outside.

And Dulcie returned with stony face and sat down, and Kate, unsmiling, carried in the stew. 'Take Father Ambrose's place away,' said Dulcie. 'Thank you, Kate. It will give us more room.'

Cautious silence emanated from the guests. There was electricity in the air. In the very curtains. Time passed. The carer thought that she would kill for a cigarette.

'If he's not coming in, Granny,' asked Herman, loud and clear, 'can I have some more stew? It's great.'

Dulcie looked at him and loved him, and there was a chorus about the excellence of the stew, and Fiscal-Smith said it was not a stew but a veritable *daube* as in the famous lunch in *To the Lighthouse*.

'I've no idea,' said Dulcie grandly. 'I bought it for freezing. From the farmers' market, months ago. I don't think I've ever been to a lighthouse.'

'Virginia Woolf couldn't have given us a stew like this. Or a *daube*,' said one of the sisters (Olga), who had once been up at Oxford.

'She wasn't much of a cook,' said the other one (Fairy). 'But you don't expect it, when people have inner lives.'

'As we must suppose', Feathers put in quickly, before Dulcie realised what Fairy had said, 'this monk has. He is certainly without inner manners.'

Everyone waited for Dulcie to say something but she didn't. Then, 'Granny, why are you crying?' and Herman ran to her and stroked her arm. 'Hey, Granny, we don't care about the monk.'

'He – he suddenly felt – indisposed and – he vanished.' Her lunch party – her reputation as the hostess on Privilege Hill – gone. They would all laugh about it for ever.

Dulcie couldn't stop imagining. She could hear the very words. '*That* brought her down a peg. Asked this VIP bishop, or archbishop, or [in time] the Prince of Wales, and he took one step inside the house and went right out again. And she'd offered to drive him to the airport. What a snob! Of course, Kate knows more than she'll say. There must be something scandalous. Drunken singing and drums. African drumming. Yes – at Dulcie's. But Kate is very loyal. They'll all be leaving her a nice fat legacy.'

'A funny business. He probably caught sight of the other guests.'

'Or the dreadful grandson.'

Etc.

Then someone would be sure to say, 'D'you think there *was* a monk? Dulcie's getting . . . well, I'll say nothing.'

'Yes, there *was* someone. Standing looking in at them over that trough of umbrellas. Some of them saw him. Dripping wet.'

'Didn't he have an umbrella himself?'

'No. I don't think they carry them. He was wearing see-through plastic. It shone. Round his head was a halo.'

'On Privilege Hill?'

'Yes. It was like Star Wars.'

'Well, it makes a change.'

The story died away. The Iraq war and the condition of the Health Service and global warming took over. The weather continued rainy. The old twins continued to drowse. The carer had home thoughts from abroad and considered how English country life is more like Chekhov than *The Archers* or Thomas Hardy or even the Updike ethic with which it is sometimes compared. She would write a paper on the subject on her return to Poland.

But the startling image of the dripping monk remained with her. She felt like posting him an umbrella.

Kate, the ubiquitous cleaner, told her friend the gardener, 'Oh yes, he was real all right. And young. And sort of holylooking.'

The gardener said, 'Watch it! You'll get like them. They're all bats around here.'

'I feel like giving him an umbrella,' Kate said. 'Wonderful smile.'

And one day Dulcie, in the kitchen alone with the gardener, Herman visiting Judge Veneering for a jam session, said, 'Don't tell anyone this, but that day, Father Ambrose in the rain, I kept thinking of Easter morning. The love that flowed from the tomb. Then the disappearance. I want to *give* him something.' She splashed gin into her tonic.

'Don't have another of those,' said the gardener to his employer.

Later, to old Feathers, who had called to present her with his dead wife's pink umbrella, having wrested it the day before with difficulty from Veneering, she said: 'I want to give him something.'

'Come, Dulcie. He behaved like a churl.'

'Oh, no. He must suddenly have been taken ill. I *did* know him, you know. We met at a day of silence in the cathedral.'

'Silence?'

'Yes. But our eyes met.'

'And he wangled a lunch and a lift?'

'Oh, didn't *wangle*. He wouldn't *wangle*. We talked for a few minutes.'

'A fast worker.'

'Well, so was Christ,' said Dulcie smugly.

Feathers, wishing he could tell all this rubbish to his dear dead wife, said, 'You're in love with the perisher, Dulcie.'

'Certainly not. And we 're all perishers. I just need to fill the blank. To know why he melted away.'

'He probably caught sight of Herman.'

'How dare you!'

'No – I mean it. Monks have to keep their distance from small boys.'

And Dulcie yearned for her dear dead husband to kick Feathers out of the house.

'I have a notion to send that . . . person in the garden

— an umbrella,' said one twin to the other. 'I shall send it to Farm Street. In London. The Jesuit HQ. "To Father Ambrose, from a friend, kindly forward to St Umbrage on Skelt."' The other twin nodded.

Fiscal-Smith, who never wasted time, had already laid his plans. On his train home to the north on his second-class return ticket bought months ago (like the stew) to get the benefit of a cheaper fare, he thought he would do something memorable. Send the monk a light-hearted present. An umbrella would be amusing. He would send him his own. It was, after all, time for a new one. And he had had a delightful day.

Staunch fellow, he thought. Standing out there in the rain.

Veneering phoned Feathers to see if Feathers would go in with him on an umbrella for that fellow at Dulcie 's on the way to the Scottish islands, the fellow who didn't turn up. Feathers said no and put the phone down. Feathers, a travelled man and good at general knowledge, had never heard of an island called Skelt or a saint called Umbrage. No flies on Judge Feathers. Hence Veneering because the pleasure of the lunch party would not leave him — the boy who liked him, the Bechstein, the drumming, the jam sessions to come

— amazed himself by ordering an umbrella from Harrods and having it sent.

Five parcels were delivered soon afterwards to Farm Street Church. One parcel had wires and rags sticking out of it. And because it was a sensitive time just then in Irish politics, and because the parcels were all rather in the shape of rifles, the Farm Street divines called the police.

Old Filth was right. The Jesuits had never heard of Father Ambrose. So they kept the umbrellas (for a rainy day, hoho) except for Fiscal-Smith's. And that they chucked in the bin.

Surge

Erin Soros

THE BUS WINDOWS rattled with the engine starting as Olaf plunked down next to his sister. The leather smelled like an old man. All the big boys sat together in the back of the school bus where they were shouting now about how they were going to climb the surge tank all the way to the top, this time they wouldn't turn chicken and creep back down. They called at Olaf, laughing and tossing a roll of caps toward his head. He pretended he couldn't hear. Pulled at the collar of his shirt, the fabric scratching his neck, and then opened his book to stare at the lines of black on white. The bus was a cage full of noise. Greta stretched over his shoulder to look back at the boys, but Olaf knew they'd be talking too fast for her to read their lips. She slipped back into the seat. Each time the bus rounded a corner, her hip dug into his thigh.

He turned to face her, stretching his lips into huge ugly shapes. "What did you do at school today, Greta?"

he asked, exaggerating each word. Before she could respond he began to sign. This time he wasn't making words. He was fluttering his fingers as fast as the wings of an insect. Greta stopped rocking her legs. Her mouth formed a small knot.

"It's a bee," he said, his voice warmer now, as if he'd been waiting all along to share this trick with his sister. "Just a bee. See Greta? The letter *B*." He pinched her under the arm until she squealed and pulled away. She giggled. Even her laugh sounded wrong.

The bus dropped off most of the children, who lived near town. Only Ralph was left. The bus creaked and huffed up a hill and around the next bend. When it braked, its metal joints complaining, Ralph walked to the front, nodded once goodbye, then was gone. The bus rocked over gullies and bumps, Olaf and Greta with their hands in their laps, surrounded by rows of green seats. Olaf stared out the window. Instead of sky, he saw hemlock and spruce, cedar and fir, the glass cloudy with Greta's breath so the trees were smeared into an unbroken green wall. *Skirttree*, Olaf signed in his lap as they passed the giant red cedar that marked the halfway point to home, its base stretching out like the sweep of a lady's skirt. His hands took the shape of what passed: the abandoned truck, the white pine burned black by lightning, the break in the woods that showed a slice of ocean, the pile of rocks where Greta scarred her knee. Each landmark he signed and Greta matched his sign

Behind these trees, closer to the shore, were the houses the Japanese families had been forced to leave behind. Greta liked to ask him what was inside – beds and tables, like their own house? But Olaf didn't want to imagine the rooms, each one dim as a shadow. Beside the busy stink of the mill town, beside their own lives in the boisterous logging camp he knew so well, the woods were full of people who were gone. From here no one could see the empty buildings, but he still felt uneasy whenever he passed this part of the road, as if the houses themselves were what made the families disappear.

Before the children were taken away, Greta had given one of the boys a ball of red yarn, just like that, something she'd stolen from home. What would he need yarn for, Olaf had asked her – a boy? He had held it tenderly, away from his body, the way one would balance a bomb. Olaf remembered his cupped hands, the knuckly fingers that were calloused from fishing like a man's would be, but sweaty and dirty from run-sheep-run.

Greta did those kinds of things. She did it without thinking about who was the enemy.

Now Olaf didn't sign their word for *house*. He looked up the road to find something else he could name.

The road narrowed and branches scratched at the windows, trying to speak. Greta leaned her head on his shoulder. They rode higher for three miles, the trees coming closer, the road darker. Then the bus stopped, and they climbed out. The driver told him to look after the little girl.

No buildings here, just the dirt road splitting the forest in two and the scrub where they hid their bikes. The logging camp was four miles farther, up the mountain on a road too steep and rough for the school bus, a single lane used for empty trucks heading up and loaded trucks heading down, the vehicles blasting warnings with their air horns at each bend in the road. The children pushed their bikes a bit, then got on to pedal, Olaf listening for oncoming trucks.

In the summertime, they stopped for huckleberries, squirting them between their teeth. They would sit at the crib dam and spit the sour ones into the tumbling water. But today the air bit their knuckles. He needed to get Greta home. He tried to yank his sleeves down over his wrists. Greta followed him a few yards back, moaning at the wind. When they reached the hill, she climbed off her bike to walk.

"I'm not walking with you," Olaf twisted around to say. "You've got to pedal." He kept his grip tight. She propped the bike against her hip so she could sign that she was tired. "Keep going," he said. "Get back on."

He was not going to get off to push both their bikes, not this time. There was nothing wrong with her arms.

All the way to the crib dam she trailed behind him, walking her bike with one hand, the frame leaning so far to the right that Olaf thought it would tip. He pedalled as slowly as he could. His bike rocked side to side, and he had to keep dropping one foot to the ground to keep it steady.

"It's getting dark!" he shouted, turning back to her, not sure if she could see his lips in the dusk. Soon they wouldn't be able to talk at all.

He crossed the crib dam — the wide concrete buttress smooth under his tires, the water clamouring far below — then stopped to let her catch up. He ducked into the bush. She trudged along. When she passed him, she didn't look up, just kept her gaze on the slow spin of her bicycle's wheel.

She turned the bend. Then he was pedalling back down the logging road, away from her, his legs spinning as furious as the sound of the water. He would be at the bottom of the hill by the time she turned around to look.

He moved faster down the main road that led back to town. When he reached the dirt bank, he found a tangle of bikes where the boys had tossed them aside. He dragged his bike up the bank and dropped it on top of the pile.

The surge tank was another mile down the trail. Only one boy had ever climbed it. Now that boy was fighting in the war.

Olaf ran into the trail that led to the beach. He could see the tank, the metal tower rising three-hundred feet. Under the darkening clouds it was whiter than usual.

He hurried, angry at the brambles and branches, stopping to catch his breath when he finally pushed through
the end of the trail where it opened onto the beach.
Even in the dusk he knew to tell apart the brown and
blue and green shapes of this coast, waves grasping at
scattered driftwood as though this flotsam could hold
the water to the shore. A log boom roofed the left side
of the bay. There were more logs scattered on the beach,
jammed end to end or crisscrossed, chewed almost hollow by torrito bugs. Boulders and stumps bordered the
miles and miles of trees, the stink of kelp vying with the
sharp pine oil.

Down by the boom the boys were tossing rocks into
the ocean, not skipping them — just lobbing handfuls of
rocks into the air and letting them drop. The boys made
bombing sounds.

"Hey," Olaf called out.

The five opened up their circle to let him stand with
them. He picked up a rock and tossed it into the water.
Waves reached up and closed around it.

"Let's go," said Joel. The boys scrambled up the beach
single file, each kicking rocks ahead, trying to hit the
nearest boy in front. Ralph stopped when he found a
good flat stone, and they all waited for him to skip it.
They counted as it bounced off the smooth water.

"Nine," Karl said, and whistled. They started walking
again, crunch of mussel shells under their soles, none of
them willing to try to beat Ralph. Olaf slipped his boots

into the others' footprints, his face hot against the cold air. He could see the surge tank clearly now. The white paint glowed like phosphorescence.

"Climbed it before?" Ralph whispered. Olaf hated him for asking in front of the other boys.

The wind was rising from the ocean and twisting past the surge tank's slick surface, making the metal ring out. As long as Olaf could remember, the tower had been here, cleaving the landscape. He knew what it was for: when the men needed to repair a turbine at the powerhouse, they had to turn off the river, funnelling all the dammed water down the mountain through the penstalk and into the tank to let gravity absorb the surge. Now the tank was empty. A great blank dividing the sky. There was the dirty white of clam shells, the flashing tips of waves. And then there was this surge tank. Even in the rain it looked clean. Olaf and Greta had walked up to its base and touched it to see if the metal was warm or cold, but they never tried the ladder. It ran from the height of the tank and then stopped eight feet from the ground.

"To the very top?" Olaf asked Ralph.

"You climb the tank first, you get to drop out of school," Ralph said.

"You can't look down," Igmar yelled. "That's what kills you."

The boys all jumped onto a line of rain-wet logs and walked along them, silent again, hands in their pockets to prove they didn't need arms to balance. The rotting wood had softened and it crumbled under their steps. They reached the tank. They crouched together to pull a small log under the ladder, then dragged another to perch on top. The second log seesawed up and down. Knut held it still while the others climbed on top. One by one they balanced on the log – leaning back and forth – gripped the ladder and pulled themselves up, scurrying fast so the next boy could join them.

Ralph stood back, picking up rocks. Olaf nodded toward the tank.

Ralph tossed a rock at it, a high ping. The boys above them stopped, looked down, then started again. Olaf and Ralph eyed each other awkwardly, Olaf tearing at a fingernail with his teeth, Ralph sliding his tongue along the cracks in his bottom lip. Knut waited, keeping the log steady.

Olaf cupped his hands together to form a holster for Ralph's foot. Ralph scattered the rest of his rocks across the sand, looked up again at the tank, then walked over to prop his foot in Olaf's palm. With a grunt Ralph hoisted himself up onto the log and leaned over to grip the ladder. He started to climb.

Salt air pushed open Olaf's lungs. His fingers were raw. He wanted to cheer on his friend. Ralph climbed a few more rungs, then Olaf reached for the ladder. He scrambled until he had his feet on it, and then he peered down at Knut who would have to climb up with no one underneath to help.

He'd been up ladders before. The first forty feet were easy. He felt a burst of energy as his boots pattered from rung to rung with a hollow clang, the ground receding beneath him. Olaf knew his father could walk up this thing easier than walking into his own kitchen.

But halfway up, the surge tank flared like a goblet, the top wider than the bottom, the sides jutting out at a thirty degree angle over the beach. Olaf had to climb not just up, but out. With his arms stretched above him, his back hung parallel to the dark sea that crashed on the shore a hundred feet below.

The weight of his body pulled at his hands. He glanced down at the water. The view swayed too fast, lurching forward then retreating as his stomach turned. He clenched his eyes shut. His left foot slipped from the ladder and flailed. This leg suddenly felt longer than the other, heavier, the muscle pulling as the foot dangled in the air. He swung forward to hook the wayward heel over the rung, found his footing, pressed his face against the ladder's cold metal edge. He breathed. He could hear Knut breathing below. The rung of the ladder felt good under his boots.

If Greta were with him, she'd want to go down.

Someone up above was laughing. At first Olaf thought one of the boys was laughing at him. Ralph had almost reached the section of the ladder where it became perpendicular again. But he was clinging to the ladder without moving. It was Ralph who was laughing, only it didn't sound like Ralph; the laugh was high-pitched and fast, and it echoed off the surge tank's metal walls.

There was something wrong with Ralph. The laugh got sharper and sharper. Ralph screeched like a crow. Olaf's arms started to shake as if he were the one laughing. A ripple of air moved through his chest.

He wouldn't laugh. He was not going to laugh.

Ralph's arms were going to loosen. Laughter would slacken his muscles.

"Keep going," Knut shouted from below.

"I can't. It's not me," Olaf said. "Ralph has stopped. It's not me."

When Olaf looked up he saw that Ralph had swung to the side of the ladder to let him pass. Ralph was still laughing, but more quietly now. His feet were jammed tight together and he was hanging on with one arm. His body swayed out like a cupboard door. Olaf clawed his fingers around the ladder's rungs, one hand over the next until he was sharing a rung with Ralph. He could keep only one boot on the ladder, tucking the other as close to the rung as he could. His left hand began to spasm. He could see the bottom of Igmar's, Joel's and Karl's boots moving higher then vanishing as the ladder straightened. A few more feet and Olaf and Ralph would reach the section where the ladder straightened to vertical. The ascent would be easier from there. Olaf opened his mouth to explain this, but something about Ralph's laugh made him stop. He wanted to climb away from it.

"Wait here," Olaf said. "Wait and we'll get you on the way down."

He climbed ahead. Looking down, he saw that Ralph was gripping the ladder again with both hands. Olaf felt lighter. The laugh coming out of Ralph faded. He knew he'd make it to the top. Olaf was stepping into the sky. Beside him a seagull rolled on the air.

He curved around the tank where the ladder straightened again, his arms stretching ahead to find the rungs. When he got his grip, he had to let both feet hang out free before he could swing them back onto the ladder as he pulled himself up, his sweating palms squeaking on the metal. He climbed another eighty feet. The half moon lit the edges of the surrounding clouds. A cobweb caught his cheek. In the last stretch of the climb, the ladder narrowed, the rungs not rounded but flat. Their edges dug into his palms. Bits of rust stuck to his hands, flaked into his eyes. He tried to keep climbing with his eyelids clamped shut, but the surge tank started to tip.

The ladder seemed too narrow for a man. Olaf wondered who climbed up here and why he did it. A seagull swooped and cawed. Olaf waved at the too-close flap of its wings.

Above him the other boys had reached the top. Knut

was a few rungs behind. Olaf couldn't hear Ralph at all.

He grabbed the last rung, swung himself up and folded his body over the edge of the roof, his arms dipping into shallow stagnant water.

The other boys watched him, Joel's face as white as the tank.

Three hundred feet. Olaf stood up.

The roof of the surge tank was as flat and white as the sides and the boys scattered like five peas on a plate. Rain had pooled on the surface. The boys all kicked at it – small explosions of water. They whacked their boots into the metal to hear it clang.

The wind answered. It sounded different than it did on the ladder, low and hollow, it didn't thud against the roof but whipped and whined across the surface as if trying to slide the boys right off. Olaf leaned into this wall that pushed at his chest. His jacket was fat with air.

There were dead birds. A seagull, dark grey and rotting, its wings splayed out in a puddle. The feathers shimmied slightly as wind raked the water. And smaller birds, a blackbird, and what he thought were chickadees, although it was hard to tell in the dark. Their bodies were clumps. They reminded him of the mousetraps in the cookhouse, the cook walking to the woods with a dustpan full of eyeless tufts of fur. Did the birds fly here to die? Or was theresomething on the roof that killed them?

Olaf looked across the water at the lumps of islands, darker black than the black of the sky, each island rimmed in purple. He was higher than any tree. His father had never been this high. Up the coast he could see the electric glow of the Powell River Mill – the light as yellow as the stink of sulphur. It lit the smoke that poured into the sky in four iridescent columns. Men were scurrying inside that box, masks over their faces as they released the spray of chemicals to turn trees into pulp. The lines of company houses were dim squares.

He turned to the south. If it were daytime, he'd be able to see all the way to Desolation Sound. A mile down the coast the moon caught the powerhouse's grey stone roof. All he could see was this roof, but he knew the front of the building had been painted to match the shore and trees, camouflage against enemy attack. The sides and back had been left as they were, the powerhouse greeting the ocean with this false face.

The Japs could attack now and Olaf could watch the planes swoop down and the incendiary bombs fall. The vibrations would rattle the surge tank and shake Ralph off the ladder. When his body landed on the beach it would snap like the sticks they held to play war. Olaf looked up the coast at the sharp blades of the tree tops. He could reach over and pluck them from the ground.

Tug boats flickered green and red and white. In daylight the boats always looked happy, bobbing in the water, nudging log booms so much larger than themselves. He could not see the boom now, but knew it was there by the way it interrupted the water's ribbon of moon.

The Japs wouldn't bomb the ocean; they'd bomb the mill. The camps. He turned around and Tin Hat Mountain stretched out behind him. The mountain was a black mass, something inked out. The logging camp where he lived was tucked behind the hill where the mountain dipped before it climbed again. He imagined his mother and sister in the wooden house. They were sitting by the stove and talking about where Olaf had gone. Across the table they passed his name back and forth. What I'm going to do to that boy, his mother said. She couldn't see him, way up here. Greta couldn't watch his hands. He stretched them up in the air.

"What's that ball for?" Joel asked him, pointing at a metal ball the size of a crouching man. It lay on top of the tank like a giant's toy.

"Lightning," Olaf said right away, and the boys nodded. His words lifted in the dark wind. "It captures lightning. It protects the surge tank." Olaf wasn't sure if this was really what it did, but the boys looked convinced. He could say anything up here and it would become true.

Olaf was the last to leave the roof. The others were kicking the birds off the tank, waiting to hear the splat and not hearing the splat so shoving at each other and asking who was scared, who was scared now, until one of them finally marched toward the ladder. Olaf watched each head disappear.

When he grabbed it, the ladder was shaking. The wind and all that space down to the ocean dragged him forward, the urge to fall. He backed away from the ladder. Sure that the others couldn't see him, he got on his hands and knees and crawled. He turned to nudge his foot down until he could feel the third rung. He held on. The flat edges dug into his palm. The wind pulled at his clothes. If he let go now, he would float.

It was harder going down, his arms and legs awkward with each backward step. His hands were growing numb. He counted as he descended. The seagulls had gone. What time was it now? He kept his eyes on his hands, dizzy with the effort not to look below. The rungs of the ladder thickened. He reached the bend where it began to run diagonal. He had to curl himself around the corner, boot searching for a rung. He hinged from the hips, kicking his feet forward so they could catch the ladder while he kept his right hand on the straight section above. With his left hand he grasped the lower part of the ladder. The rust made his grip slide. To continue down, he was going to have to let go of his upper hand. He released his fingers, each one still frozen around the shape of the rung. He reached below for the ladder. His hand opened and closed on air. He was falling backward. Then his fingers smacked the metal and he clasped the rung tight. His whole body began to tremble. Upside down in the sky.

Ralph was still there. As Olaf climbed slowly toward him, swaying his feet forward with each step so he could catch the next rung, he could see Ralph's arms rigid against the ladder. The laughing had stopped. Olaf had swallowed a flake of rust and it tickled his throat. He coughed. It sounded like a laugh.

Ralph hooked one arm over the rung and one arm under it and leaned closer in.

"Ralph Forrest," Olaf said. The name ricocheted off the surge tank.

The wind tugged at Ralph's hair and flapped his jacket open. Olaf wondered if he had seen the birds the boys kicked off. Ralph squeezed to one side of the ladder so Olaf could pass.

Olaf climbed down until the two boys perched on the same rung, boots cramped in a line. Ralph pressed his cheek against the ladder.

"Go on," Olaf said. Below them there was the steady hollow clang of boots hitting metal. The other boys had climbed past Ralph. Were they going for help? The wind whistled through the ladder and whipped Ralph's hair across his eyes.

"Go on."

Ralph didn't move. The boys were nearing the bottom. Olaf dropped one foot to the next rung.

He waited. Ralph glanced down, snot running into

his mouth. He wouldn't let go of the ladder long enough to wipe it away. His sleeve slipped to the elbow to reveal his arm taut with muscle and veins. Olaf could still reach out and rest his palm on the nape of Ralph's neck to coax him down, but he didn't want to touch Ralph.

"Say something. Ralph. Talk. It will make it better." Bits of his words were torn by the wind.

Olaf waited.

Even the jaunty under-the-breath comments Ralph always made, even those he'd take.

Come on.

Go on.

Ralph was not going to move.

Olaf took another step down. He felt Ralph watch him. Three more steps, four, and he looked up through the black shapes of Ralph's boots. If Ralph let go without leaping free of the tank, his body would crash straight down and tear Olaf from the ladder and they both would drop to the earth.

As he neared the bottom, he climbed more quickly, careful not to look down until he was close enough to jump. Three yards from the ground, he leapt free with a high-pitched yell. He cleared the logs, landed on the balls of his feet, then rolled into the familiar crunch of sand and shells. He lay there for a moment, feeling the moist sand flat between his shoulder blades. Above the clouds, the stars looked as if someone had thrown a handful of rocks across the sky.

Ralph was still on the surge tank, but smaller. He hadn't moved. If Olaf didn't know Ralph was there, he wouldn't realise the dark speck was a boy.

Olaf scurried to his feet, rubbed shells and pebbles off his knees.

"You coming?" Karl yelled as he ran toward the water. The other boys ran too, jumping up and down on beach logs. The salt air was sharp on Olaf's face. Down by the ocean, the boys began to shout.

"Dumplings and gravy! Right now a whole plateful of dumplings and gravy!"

"Roast beef!"

Olaf couldn't tell who was saying what. His stomach spasmed. It was long past dinner. Greta and his mother would be eating without him. Greta would ask if she could have his portion and his mother would blow cigarette smoke across the table, say she always knew her son would do something like this, then slide his plate to Greta.

"No, flapjacks. A foot-high stack of flapjacks!"

"And bacon!"

"And bacon! Hey Ralph! We're going to have bacon!"

"Pork and beans!" one of them bellowed over the noise of the waves.

That's what Olaf wanted. They could stay out here all night and sit around a bonfire like the men do in the summer, heat a can over the flames. Ralph would climb down, shoulder Olaf for a space, grab a spoon. They wouldn't say how long he'd been up there. They'd eat. Olaf would have liked his tin lunch box right now, its slim black handle. He'd unfold his mother's wax paper and pass her bread pudding to the boys.

"Salmonberry pie!" Olaf heard his voice toss the words out into the wind. He was suddenly giddy. "Salmonberry pie!" He yelled up to Ralph as if he had a piece to offer. He could do this. He could just shout out what he wanted to eat.

Olaf turned to see where the boys were. They'd almost reached the trail that led to the road. If he didn't go now, he'd lose them.

"Salmonberry pie!" he shouted at the surge tank before breaking into a run.

When they reached the road, the other boys climbed onto the pile of bikes to rip out their own. Olaf was still running through the trail, but he could see the flicker of wheels through the trees. He caught up. They saluted Olaf and he saluted them back. He grabbed his bike. Ralph's bike was lying by itself. The tyre was close to the road and Olaf thought maybe they should push it toward the trail. The other boys wheeled off. The wind died down. His bike felt cold and wet. Without Greta to slow him, he'd be home in no time.

He pedalled back up the logging road. He flew into the camp and lifted his hands off the handlebars. The bike pitched to the left and he swayed his weight to the right and kept pedalling without holding on. The cook-house was dark; the bunkhouses were dark; the men weren't sitting outside smoking or spitting tar. No one could see him now.

He careened along the trail to his home. Without taking off his boots, he walked through the back door and across the linoleum, pleased with the mud tracks, the wet slap of his soles on the floor. The kitchen was empty.

The air smelled of stale smoke. He checked the stove. The pots were full of food that hadn't been served.

Balls of wool sat on the chesterfield, pierced by knitting needles, and he wished now for their comforting click, clack, his mother's sighs as she worked.

He leaned against the airtight heater to feel its warmth. Someone must be home. It was dangerous to leave a roaring fire when no one was home.

He stopped to listen. Rustle of fire in the airtight. Click of the pane against the frame. The wind had started blowing again, but more gently. He could hear his own breath, his blood pounding in his ears, the flick of his fingernail tearing at the skin of his cuticles. His steps were too loud as he walked slowly toward the stairs, heel to toe, his arms stiff by his side as if he were trying to find his balance.

A house has a face – from outside, but even from inside he could tell that the two windows above the sink were blank as untelling eyes. When he was a small boy, he used to be afraid of the house — not the creak of the stairs or the wind in the attic or even his bedroom closet where someone, something, could hide — he was afraid of the windows themselves, the glass that held the glowing light from the lamp, and these wooden walls that were as thick as a man's shoulders are broad. He thought the house could watch him, when he did something wrong, that it knew things that even his mother did not.

But the stairs tonight were reassuring to climb, each step wide enough for his boots, his hand holding this familiar cedar banister that his father had sanded smooth and round as a candle. He wondered if Ralph was still gripping the ladder's slick rungs. When he reached the top of the stairs, he kept hold of the banister and clenched his eyes shut as if this would stop Ralph from letting go. Now he wanted to make a noise, cough or call out, anything to fill the house. He thumped his hand on the doorframe as he marched into his parents' room — dark. Into Greta's room, rapping first on the open door although she wouldn't be able to hear. Moonlight caught a book splayed on the floor, a page lifting on its own. Beside the book was one of the Red Ryder comics Greta liked to sneak from Olaf.

He sat on the unmade bed. He would give Greta the comic book, to keep, when she came home. The promise tightened its grip on his thoughts the way tangled sheets bind sleep.

He could give one comic to Greta and one to Ralph. No – more than one. He would let them have as many as they wanted. Handing over his prized collection filled him with a sharp pleasing sense of loss.

The wind rattled the glass against the frame. Underneath him were Greta's heavy woollen blankets, he could lie down, fall asleep, feel the rush of relief he always felt on waking up from a bad dream.

Outside, in the distance, his mother was calling him. He pressed his boots firmly into the floor to hold her voice in place.

She called again. He scurried downstairs and out the front entrance. The air was colder now that he'd been inside. He left the door open and light spilled a jagged yellow triangle over the steps. He ran through the trail. Up ahead, there was a thin white shimmer between the trees. His mother was standing alone outside in her nightgown, the bulk of her overcoat hanging awkwardly over it. When she saw Olaf, she ran toward him, almost tripping as she opened her arms.

"Greta!" she called out, "Greta!" He wanted to shrink into his sister's name.

His mother held him and he buried his face into the slick softness of the nightgown. "Greta – where is she? Is she back at the house? Olaf? Is she with you? Olaf? Where is your sister?" His eyelashes flickered against her warm chest. As long as he didn't answer her questions, he could keep his arms around her. "Greta?"

she asked again. Her body stiffened.

"Mom, I didn't..."

"What did you do?"

"Mom, she..."

She pushed past him to run up the trail. He watched the back of her overcoat.

"She ran away," he yelled. His mother stopped. She turned to face him. Her coat swung open and again he could see the white flicker of her nightgown. "Greta raced down the road on her bike, before I knew where she was going, before I could catch her, she wouldn't do what I said, she wouldn't look, she wouldn't stop, she went speeding on her bike down the logging road, I couldn't see where she went."

"Greta...Greta did?" She walked back, her feet careful over stones and broken branches.

"I've...I've been looking for her. I didn't come home. I've been looking for Greta for hours." The lie stretched out to his mother and pulled her toward him.

"Where did you look?" she asked. Her voice was softer now. "The men have split up. They're all searching. Did you see your father?"

"The beach," he blurted out. He felt as light as he did on top of the surge tank. He could say anything. "I looked for her at the beach." His mother nodded. She gazed out past his head. She pressed her hands together like she was praying, but she wasn't praying. Olaf took her arm, the bone under her nightgown under her coat, and led her back to the house.

Not until he shuffled her to the table – slipped off her coat, pulled out the cups for tea, put the kettle on the stove, slid her tobacco in front of her so she could roll a cigarette – did he realise that he knew where his sister had gone.

He walked outside and grabbed his bike, turned to see his mother standing in the light of the doorway. She looked afraid, the lamplight shining through her gown and silhouetting her legs. "Olaf," she cried. He liked her saying his name. He started to pedal down the path and she called it once more.

He careened down the logging road, then onto the main road that led to the surge tank, keeping his eyes on the spin of his front wheel. The ladder was on the other side of the tank, facing the ocean, so he couldn't see Ralph even if he looked.

The men were combing the shore. Olaf strained to track their voices. The loggers called out for his sister, then for him. His father led each call then the other voices joined in. The shouts trailed off and all the men stood silent as they waited for a response. Their bodies were still, black as paper cut-outs against the ocean's tumble. The woods absorbed the echo. Then the men began calling again, sway of lanterns etching the trees. Olaf imagined running down to show them he was safe – he'd throw his arms wide and announce where Greta had gone, spill the news like light. His father's face would lift, smile, he'd nod as if Olaf had made her appear.

He jumped off and pushed his bike to where the woods thinned. The men were small, visible only between the dark columns of firs. In the mist rising from the ocean, their lanterns bobbed like small floating moons.

They were nearing the surge tank. Light swung up against its surface. Someone had begun to carry a lantern up the ladder. Olaf dropped his bike and pushed his way past the trees, arching his head back to see the tower swooping into the sky so that the swirl of dark clouds seemed to be underneath his body instead of high above it – the sky was the ocean, the surge tank rocking in the waves. He had to grip a branch to steady himself.

Ralph was still holding on.

Olaf grinned and wrapped his arms around his chest, rubbing his hands up and down to get the blood moving. He thought of Ralph's hair lifting in the wind.

With a shiver he realised that the climbing man was his own father, the familiar wide shoulders rising quickly up and up and it was strange now to see his father chart the same height that Olaf himself had climbed, his father's body so high and yet shrunken against the expanse of white – a man crouching down to join a boy's game. His father's steps were too heavy, his boots would shake the rungs and make the remaining birds fall from the top of the tank, wingless carcasses dropping the length of the tower like secrets, each one landing in a waterlogged splat.

The birds were dead already. Olaf was not responsible for the birds.

Ralph had managed to climb down to where the tank ran vertical again but now he had stopped. He was waiting for Olaf's father. Olaf had seen his father climb this high many times before. His father could reach this high or higher each time he rigged a new spar tree, climbing it and then topping it and wrapping the guyline confidently around the tree's tip as tight as a noose. He could climb the spar while waving down at Olaf, then reach the top and smoke a cigarette and take off his hat and pass it through the air as if collecting rain and even as he sat on the flat top of the tree without his belt roping him to it, even as he perched with nothing to hold him to the trunk's quivering height running straight down to the ground that lay so solid under Olaf's feet, his father was tipping his hat to him and so his father was attached to him and would not fall.

Now his father was hatless, hand over hand to reach another man's son. He did not turn to wave.

When his father reached Ralph, he plucked the boy's fingers from their tight grip on the rungs and wrapped the boy's arms around his shoulders. From the ground Olaf could no longer see Ralph. His black shape had disappeared inside the man's so that they moved as a single body.

Olaf got back on his bike, pedalling fast through the trees that swayed toward his face until he feared he'd lose his balance. The sound of the wheels mimicked the crying sounds he imagined Ralph would make. The men would wrap him in one of their Mack jackets. The men would offer him a sip of moonshine from one of the flasks they kept in their canvas satchels and then Olaf's father would lean down to speak to the boy at his own level, gazing into his eyes the way he looked into Olaf's whenever he wanted the truth.

There's a look a child gets when he has something good to tell, when he knows something valuable that an adult wants. At first Ralph would say nothing, letting the moonshine dilate the blood vessels in his fingers and his feet. Olaf knew that warm sensation. Olaf had come in from the cold to feel his frozen fingers softening and opening as soon as his father's whiskey was in him, as if his hands and not his mouth had drunk the amber brew. To sit like that with his father beside the airtight, warmth outside his skin and inside his skin – Olaf would have told him anything.

Now Olaf turned down another trail a mile north of the surge tank toward the cragged beach where the boats and houses sat unused. The woods swallowed him. Then the forest exploded with music, one high-pitched voice then something like a fiddle. His bike rattled over branches, in the dark he couldn't see the forest floor. With each bounce the music tried to shake him off. The trail opened onto the beach.

Every window of the Jap house was lit. The building was leaning slightly toward the ocean, close to the water like a beached boat, squares of light doubled by a rippled reflection.

The music was coming from inside, the volume cranked so high that the windowpanes were shaking, sound tinny and broken. The house's slanting walls seemed too fragile to hold it.

A lull in the music. He heard Greta, her low rocking voice. Her singing slid left and right of the tune. She flitted by the glass. The flames of oil lanterns followed her wake. He dropped his bike and crept to the house to watch her as she swooped back and forth across his view, a flash of blue that appeared, disappeared, dancing from one end of the kitchen to the other, her hair a swirl of light around her head as she leapt from a stool into the air

He pressed his face to the glass and felt the vibrations of the music the way she would, the pulse vibrating his jaw.

She landed in a heap of blue satin. Lanterns flickering all around her, on the table, the counter, the floor. The robe covered her body like a tarp, spilled over her feet, shiny blue with red piping and red pictures stitched down the sides, small houses and smaller people and enormous curving fish. Greta grasped the satin, then she was up again, swooping around the kitchen in this robe that skimmed over the jerky quickness of her limbs. As she brushed past the table, a sleeve caught at a rice bowl and dragged it to the table's edge.

The bowl didn't fall. Greta swayed her head back and forth to the vibrations of the record, her mouth slack. No words in her singing. It bothered Olaf, the sounds that meant nothing, her low voice flooding this house where she didn't belong. The family that had lived here had been lined up with the others, bussed out, without a chance to pack their things.

Greta reached her arms up and spun in place. The robe twisted at her feet. Its long red tie whipped a lamp. The robe was going to catch on fire. He banged at the window. The latch was jammed shut. She kept dancing. He ran around to the other side of the house to reach the door.

The night air rushed in as he entered the room. Greta stood still. She didn't jump or call out. She stood with her back to Olaf. He couldn't see her expression, couldn't tell if she knew it was him. The record kept turning, the robe corkscrewed around Greta's legs.

He walked toward her. He thumbed the lantern to the middle of the table, the bowl away from the edge. There was another bowl lying mouth-down on the counter, the shards of a plate on the floor. The cupboard doors were open. Across the table she had shaped the letter *B* from grains of rice.

"Greta, it's me." He tugged at the robe. She signed

something to him, but the sleeves covered her hands. He felt her fingers flicker against the satin.

She spun from his grasp, climbed onto the counter and tore open a box of crackers, waving it in front of his face like some toy she had stolen and wouldn't give back.

You left me, her lips shaped the words as she stuffed crackers into her mouth. She swayed her head side to side.

I was there, Olaf signed.

Gone, she signed back.

I was there. It was you. You didn't see me. But his hands were small and tight: even his fingers didn't believe him. The music stopped — vinyl crackle and static. The kitchen was white with silence. Then the roar of water as the ocean hit the shore.

She said something, but she kept eating and the crackers muffled the shape of her words. His stomach clenched at the sight of food, but he wouldn't take a thing left behind by the family. Through the bedroom door, he could see another lantern, records strewn across the bed. He slipped a bowl from the counter and put it back on the table, slid the other bowl to meet it, the clink of china ringing out as the two rims touched.

Gone gone gone, she signed, shimmied down from the cupboard and traipsed around the kitchen with her hands forming the words wider and wider. But she wasn't upset. She was grinning now. Olaf would like her to be upset. He would like her to sit down.

We could stay gone all night. We could sleep here.

"We have to go home." His voice cracked. "Mom is waiting for us."

Gone gone gone. She spun around as she signed.

She swooped by Olaf again and he grabbed her by the waist, expecting her to squirm against his grip. Like a dead weight she collapsed into his chest. He held this feeling, her leaning against him, him bracing her, him keeping her from falling, if he stepped away she'd slump to the floor. "I'm here," he whispered. He mouthed the words against her cheek. She was breathing fast from the dancing, but she let him hold her, the way one of the camp whiskey jacks will step forward to peck at a palm full of seeds offered by an owner who has been gone too long. Through the slick satin Olaf was relieved to feel the rough nubs of her sweater underneath.

When he released Greta, the warmth of her body fell away from his. She stepped free of the robe, letting it drop to the floor. He bent down to pick it up, walking into the other room to place it on the bed, folded on top of the records. Two of the records were chipped, another had been cracked. He hoped it wasn't Greta who did it. He couldn't tell which broken parts were new.

She watched him shut each cupboard door in the kitchen, the flat warm sound of wood on wood. One by one he blew out the lanterns. The rooms shrunk.

Greta took his hand and swung it as they walked out the door. This bothered him too, the music in her arms, and when they reached his bike, he turned to check the house. The windows were dark. He let Greta sit on his seat and he stood up to pedal. When they had almost reached the logging road he began to get tired and he remembered that she must have ridden her own bike to the Jap house but it was too late now to go back. Her hands gripped his waist and the bike rocked with the effort of his legs as he followed the narrow track his wheels had left.

The Names
Adam Thorpe

TODAY, I SMASHED the bottle.

I drove out at dawn (though the sun had never set) to a fold of the mountains near Kiruna, to a spot the Sami traditionally hold sacred, and placed the bottle on a rock and shot it to smithereens with my father's hunting gun. I was careful to collect the fragments in a plastic bag, for fear the deer might catch them in their hoofs.

I slipped the fragments into a bin by the station. Judging from the hollow crash, the bin was empty. I cut my forefinger, but it is not serious.

We know so little about anything, but no one believes this. If only people would believe this one simple truth, we might begin again, like a proper dawn.

***

When the SS troops came into Valdaron, looking for the Resistance boys in Camp IV, they asked if someone could take them to the farmhouse called Les Pins. More precisely, they booted open the door of the café and pointed their guns into the silence. Then the captain barked out the request in poor French, mispronouncing the name.

They emerged from the café with Hubert Cros, aged nineteen. Hubert worked at the tannery on the river at St Maurice. The reason he was not in Germany as a forced labourer was his right hand: it was withered. He had been born like that. You have no idea how long it took me to discover that fact.

Hubert was a meek young man, who had spent most of his short life putting up with jibes about his deformity. His greatest wish was to wake up one morning with a perfect right hand. He was not a member of the Resistance; many locals viewed the Resistance, in any case, as a band of left-wing troublemakers, disturbers of whatever peace had been left by the occupying forces. He kept his head down, something his nineteen years had already taught him to do.

But he did know the area as well as anyone – he knew its thickest woods, its obscurest paths, its highest peaks. Like most men in Valdaron, he hunted. He had hunted with his father from the age of seven. He also set bird-traps. Despite this activity, one can say that he loved nature. He loved it because it took him away from those who found in him a butt for their jokes and into a world in which he could feel proud to be who he was. He liked to stand in a wood, alone and free, until peace had settled on it again. Then the rustlings and the birdsong would start to return, and he would feel a contentment he felt nowhere else.

Being Swedish, brought up in Varmland, I can understand this feeling for the forest; even to the extent of still sensing the possibility of bears, when the only bears in Varmland are now in the zoo. Maybe what I am sensing is the bears' collective phantom, as one senses the dead on an old battlefield. I can still hear my father telling visitors: if you see a bear, sing. If it carries on coming towards you, lie down in a foetal position.

Not every danger in life can be so treated, alas. Least of all death itself.

***

The Germans drove with Hubert up the long trackway that runs along the side of a range of hills from the top of which, on a clear day, you can see both the Alps and the Mediterranean. I doubt that any of the soldiers knew this, or were interested: I have no real idea what was passing through the minds of those men as they made their way in half-track troop carriers to the farmhouse. Perhaps fear, perhaps hatred, perhaps something we will never understand but that sits, dark and dreadful, in all of us.

One thing I do know: they had set out from their base in Nîmes at two o'clock in the morning, with the rest of the 9th Panzer Division, Waffen-SS. It was February, the cold made worse by the driving rain. They had penetrated deeply into a confusing labyrinth of dark green hills and mountains, from which at any moment they could expect bullets or explosives from the hundreds or even thousands of concealed terrorists. In reality, of course, there was only a ragtag scattering of unshaven young men, whose main method of keeping warm was to scratch at their fleas.

I also imagine that every bump and bend in the rough, unmetalled roads was an irritation to these troops, driving vehicles that were superior to the terrain, that crushed everything in their path with their caterpillar tracks and huge front tyres, that were made to be driven with a certain amount of willed aggression so that a tight curve was almost an insult to them, perched high above the ordinary world of muddle and compromise. I believe these vehicles altered those in them for the worse, as cars and most especially the four-by-four type do, of which we have so many in Sweden, and which are for me the very symbol of an inhuman capitalism.

And given these men were already aggressive, and without the ability to empathise with others (the most important human quality, to my mind), then the picture was already looking very grim for Hubert, and for the Resistance boys in Camp IV.

***

It was a journey of some five kilometres from the village.

Hubert Cros must have been very frightened as the troop-carriers approached the Mas des Pins on its steep mountainside, their engines fuming and roaring, their bulk sending out sheets of water whenever they hit the large puddles. There was very little chance for him to escape, despite his intimate knowledge of the terrain; it is usually more dangerous to try to escape. He had no choice but to obey.

It was not only very cold and wet, but misty with it. The rain, soaking the narrow valleys for days, had turned them into dark, cloud-webbed gorges, almost Amazonian in appearance. Perhaps the others in the vehicle were making jokes that, knowing no German, Hubert couldn't understand: jokes about his withered hand, or his blood-drained face, or the tannery smell on his clothes, or the look he had about him (in their eyes) of a simple peasant. Trapped under the vehicle's tarp in a dark fug of wet collars and soaking boots, squeezed between those long grey winter cagouls and their hard-eyed owners, jolted and swayed by the violent movement of the vehicle and with a gun pointed at his belly, Hubert would have been visibly shivering, of that I am in no doubt.

At some point – probably when the winding path up to the mas left the main track – the convoy stopped and men poured out, running and crouching as in all the war films or documentaries you have ever seen, their impermeable hoods up against the rain so that, in the mist, they might have been spectres, or mad monks.

Hubert was forced to run with them, his hair streaming. I know this because I have interviewed one of those present, living comfortably in a village near Düsseldorf until his death in 2001. He barely remembered the incident, I have to say, but was in no doubt that Hubert would not have been treated with much – 'patience', was the word he used, as he served me more coffee with an elderly, mottled hand, his wife hovering with the hazelnut buttercream torte.

Well, if our young hostage was showing extreme nervousness, explained the former SS soldier in a simple German I could understand, that would have made things worse: nerves are not only infectious but something to be despised, something that awakens the weakness in oneself (the weakness that was in these men especially, being the hidden shadow of the bully – although my own informant was thin and elderly and nothing like a bully, apart from a certain obstreperousness and a way of cutting the delicious torte to his advantage).

Which is why they could shoot innocent people –

even small children and old women – in cold blood. Some of these very men sitting with Hubert had already done so, most likely – if not in France then in Yugoslavia, where this particular SS division had gobbled up shawled peasants and their simple, thatched homes for breakfast, lunch and supper.

So when the vehicles stopped at the beginning of the path and the troops began to fan out up the flank of the wooded mountain, wiping the rain from their faces and wondering when the farmhouse would come into view, Hubert would have been gripped by a firm hand in case he tried to flee. It was always possible, after all, that he had misled them, that he had brought them somewhere harmless, wasting more of their precious time! Where was this farmhouse, anyway?

Then it came into view through the trees: big-stoned, tiny-windowed, added to over unrecorded generations so that it resembled an untidy accumulation of rocks.

It was empty.

It had been empty, purely coincidentally, for two days. The boys were on a mission elsewhere. The only trace of them was beds of bracken in the upper rooms; peelings of vegetables; a lingering smell of roasted chestnuts; a few charred logs in the vast fireplace. (They were to return two days later, to the blackened mess the SS had made of the place.)

Hubert had no idea the farmhouse would be empty.

Neither did he know whether it was an active camp (the Resistance kept moving camps, anyway) or an occasional hideout. He had not volunteered for this task, he had been volunteered by someone else present in the café. It is not true, as several in the village have related to me, that he was at first taken away to the commandeered police station and beaten with fists until he agreed to show them. That is a version spun from misunderstanding or forgetfulness, and which breeds even more distorted versions, mostly related by those too young to have been there at all during the war.

What had happened was this: the Germans had burst into the café, the room had fallen silent, the SS officer had demanded a guide to show them the quickest way to the Mas des Pins (there were many obscure farmhouses hidden in the hills, this was only sensible); and after a brief pause, broken only by the officer threatening terrible reprisals, one of the men in the café turned his head towards Hubert at the bar and said, 'Hubert?'

Just that. Nothing more. It was not premeditated. It was not the product of malice. It was just that everyone else on that particular afternoon in the one café in Valdaron — except for fat-bellied Auguste with his greasy apron, behind the bar, who was to be arrested a quarter of an hour later and released the next day — was well over sixty years of age and drunk.

***

They had been celebrating Aimé's birthday, which that year fell on a Saturday. Aimé was eighty-eight, the *doyen* of the village. He was born in 1856. This seems scarcely credible, somehow: that a man who witnessed the Second World War should already have been a lad of thirteen when the Franco-Prussian War broke out. Aimé would recall the return of his father from that war, and his own son's return from the trenches, minus a lung. Aimé himself was too young for one, and too old for the other. That was good luck. What was bad luck was that he lived long enough to meet the Nazis.

Aimé had fetched a wine bottle from a cupboard in his cellar: it did not contain its original wine, however, but fig brandy — so old it must have quadrupled in strength. He vaguely remembered preparing it one summer before the war — the 14-18 war, that is. The bottle was covered in dust and cobwebs through which its defiant label described an even earlier vintage, and the figs still floated about like laboratory specimens in liquid so dark they were discernible only as shadows. This was a time of want, when most of the wine in the area was being trucked off to Germany. So the men tucked into the long-fermented fig brandy with a certain lack of caution after as good a lunch as they could manage, given the shortages. By the time the SS officer and his troops burst into the café, only Hubert — who had arrived shortly before — was entirely sober. Aimé had been singing and recounting tales, his missing teeth interspersing his words with a whistle for which he was famed. The whistle grated on everyone's ears, but he himself seemed unaware of this trait.

At first, when this fact about the celebration was revealed to me, I found it interesting that ordinary life pursued its course when the SS were known to be in the vicinity. The village shops were open, the baker's son was plastering a ceiling in the bakery, dishes were being washed and dried after lunch, patched clothes ironed above the post office.

When I ventured a question on this subject at the beginning of my research over twenty years ago, I was told that up until then, in Valdaron at least, only the Wehrmacht had visited and on just one occasion, and that many of those in that particular group had been Armenian. They took a few chickens and were well-behaved. That was in 1943.

Furthermore, I learned that all those who might have feared arrest had, that morning in February 1944, fled the village, a mere three or four hours after the Waffen SS arrived in the foothills. Thus the village had only a semblance of normality, a mask. This, I think, must have irritated the tired, harrassed soldiers of the SS even more, because I am sure they would have known it was a mask — just as, whenever I ask my young language students back home in Sweden what they would like to change in their life, even the most troubled teenagers merely shrug and say something silly to amuse the others. I tell them quite candidly that what I would like to change in my life is my own cowardice.

Having smashed the bottle, what will I tell them now?

***

The group of about twelve in the café – which included Aimé's three sons, all in their sixties – were merry. Their laughter must have been audible from Valdaron's long, narrow street. The noise of the armoured vehicles and most of all the rasping motorcycles would have made the men pause, look at each other in concern, fall silent. The acoustics of the main street of Valdaron are such that a single car makes a kind of subdued booming sound below the engine noise, and this sound carries either way for a considerable distance. Assuming a fleet of some twenty armoured vehicles and ten outriding motorcycles, the noise they made must have been something akin to a roll of thunder turning cacaphonic.

Perhaps the officer had been aware of the laughter, somehow, hanging in the air just long enough for him to note its abrupt disappearance. The armoured convoy did not drive up to the café, which was (and still is) a hundred yards beyond the main square. So it is possible that the officer and a handful of men approached the café on foot while the laughter continued unawares, baiting them with its lack of concern, its insouciance.

We Swedes have so little notion of what modern warfare is really like, how it infiltrates the crevices, the details, the very joints of ordinary life.

I imagine the door was kicked open, anyway, but maybe not in the way one sees it in films. There is so little I believe in films, because in real life quite extraordinary contradictions take place that no filmgoer would ever put up with. For instance, I once saw a man shot in the head with a pellet gun in broad daylight. This was in Stockholm, but it might have been anywhere, in any city – it was a drugs-related affair between rival gangs. In a film, the onlookers (the extras, hired for the day) would have been told to look scared, or to run away, or to take cover, or even to scream. In real life, as I watched them, they looked no more than slightly anxious. And then I realised that my own expression was precisely the same as theirs. It was not a dream: the blood was still there in the morning, trapped in the ice like petals, just as the face of Lucille is trapped in my heart.

Destroying the bottle has made no difference to that, at least. Or not for the moment. I live in hope of a thaw.

***

Lucille.

In 1975, I was a student in my third year reading French and Russian at the University of Stockholm, traversing the French countryside on a mobilette bought in Paris. I had reached the mountains of the Cévennes, an area I knew little about except that it was a refuge for many of the student radicals of the sixties protest movement, who sought to put their communitarian, anti-materialist ideas into practice by herding goats or throwing pots. This is not the place to recount my minor adventures on this 50cc odyssey, except to say that as I journeyed down through those wild southerly mountains I fell in love with them.

By the time I reached the area around Valdaron, only a few days from the start of the autumn semester, I was determined to return here, possibly for good. I, too, was something of a radical idealist – like my mother. Unlike my mother, I was not a Communist. I had rebelled against her orthodoxies and gone my own way. She scoffed at my 'back-to-earth', hippy tendencies (as did my Estonian-Jewish teacher-father), accusing me of being a spoilt bourgeois, or even quasi-fascist. I believed, for instance, that all cars should be banned. This regressive attitude infuriated my parents. I was not happy in Sweden, for all its political idealism and its peaceful neutrality and its endless forests and its beautiful cities. It was too melancholy and sensible. France offered me an alternative in which my romantic tendencies could find succour (I hardly need to say that this belief would turn out to be something of a deception).

Valdaron struck me as being not only authentically

old but rather attractively shabby. That day, the village square had been given over to one of those local jumble sales they call, in France, *Vide Grenier*, or Attic Emptying; this increased the impression of shabbiness, if anything.

A bottle was standing on one of the many trestle tables, along with a motley assortment of wares that some would find anthropologically interesting, others would call rubbish, and only an artist or an eccentric would actually buy, and which included everything from the old type of electric plug to a hideous badger-trap.

This bottle interested me primarily because I needed a lampstand for my student room. Any qualms about returning to Sweden with an empty bottle (my plan was to sell the mobilette in Marseilles and return to Stockholm by train) were swiftly subdued by the added sense I had that this one object would return me by association to this place, this moment, and to France in general: much more than a souvenir! This feeling was helped, no doubt, not only by the sunlight warm on my cheek after a cold night in my hammock, but by the presence of the wonderfully good-looking girl behind the trestle table.

The bottle was evidently old enough to have been hand-blown, with a thick, uneven base and a rough bulge at the top. The label had been scribbled over on a February day near the end of the war. I handled the bottle with a feigned lack of interest. The girl behind the

trestle table was smiling at me. I am a typical Swede –
tall, blonde and slightly stern in expression, or perhaps
serious would be a kinder term – and in 1975 I was not
yet twenty. I was also tanned and a little wild-looking
by this stage of my trip, with hay in my hair.

Suffice to say we had a charming discussion, during
which I discovered that she was the great-great-niece of
the original owner of the bottle, who had lived all his
life in the village, but she could not say why the label
had a dozen signatures on it, or what the significance
of the date was, and she could not ask her grandmother, Aimé's niece, because her grandmother was dead,
and her mother was at work right now and probably
wouldn't know anyway, she didn't like all these '*vieilles
tripailles*'. I thought it was strange and amusing, calling
this sea of bric-à-brac 'old innards', as if pulled from the
living instead of barns and houses.

I say 'signatures', but at second glance it was clear
that the names had been written in full as carefully as
one can write anything on a confined, curving space
and with a fine-nibbed ink pen.

The form of the letters evoked in me a rush of nos-
talgia for a world I had never known, but since then I
have discovered that French schoolchildren still learn a
similar form of old-fashioned handwriting. Perhaps it is
for this kind of singularity that I love France so much. I
found out a little about Aimé himself, but since the girl
– called Lucille – had missed knowing him by some ten

years, this was of no real use.

When I put my nose to the top (which amused Lucille greatly) I smelt a scent of such potency (although in reality it was very faint) that I wanted to laugh. I think I did laugh, in my sober Swedish way. I was the first Swede that Lucille had ever met, and she was impressed – most of all by my French. She had dark, shining eyes and long straight brown hair that fell into natural curls like springs over her ears, and a mouth I feel only French women possess, the lips shaped by the language to a permanent, teasing pout that can look either vain or inviting, and which reminds me of a bird in flight. Lucille's pout was inviting – and beyond it, when it spread into a smile, I saw slightly crooked but very white teeth. She asked me why I didn't have a bicycle instead of a mobilette, and I told her the truth: a bicycle would be far too healthy.

'Oh,' she said, 'I thought Swedes were very keen on being healthy.'

'That's why I am not keen on being healthy,' I laughed.

She stared at me with a puzzled, uncertain look. I bought the bottle for small change and said goodbye. I was shy and had no notion of seduction. Whatever powers I had were paralysed, anyway, by the way she looked at me straight in the eye – as French girls always do, so fearlessly, even with no intention at all to flirt.

***

It was another thirteen years before I returned to that area. Meanwhile, the bottle standing on a shelf in my various digs in Sweden (I, too, was now a teacher, against all my expectations), had become my talisman. I had not turned it into a lamp, or at least not literally, not outwardly.

We all have a period in our lives in which we seem to achieve the miracle of becoming a different person, something approaching the ideal of ourselves. At least, that is the illusion. It can last days, weeks or months. Rarely more than that. For some it lasts the length of a night, or even the two hours of a great concert or play. The bottle, Lucille's bottle (as I called it), was the means by which I entered that time I journeyed through France, alone, talking to myself over the whine of the mobilette, choosing the obscurest minor roads, sleeping rough or in youth hostels that were mostly empty, arriving in a town without, in those days, having to pass through the cancerous outer ring of the so-called 'commercial zone' established everywhere now, all over Europe, in the garish, big-box American style.

Back then there were only small, brick-built factories or petrol stations, or yards where you could see people in overalls at work – proper manual work. I was happy, I was hopeful, I was a solitary Swede with the answers to all the world's problems. I assumed humanity – especially the younger strain – was mostly benevolent, courageous and good, and that the villains were easily identifiable. I assumed the future would be ours, my generation's, and that my generation was not selfish and greedy, driving the world into the wall faster and faster, as we have turned out to have done, or to be doing, in connivance with our parents and our grandparents and even those younger than us.

And gradually, over the years, I became fascinated by the faded names scribbled on the label, and knew them all by heart. I saw into their characters by dint of following the patterns their lines made, and needed to know who they were, and why they were on the bottle, although I guessed it must have been in honour of a special occasion – a birthday or perhaps a marriage. And I felt privileged, in my grey Swedish room, to have this lens of private, sunlit France through which I could see a pair of dark, shining eyes.

Although, by now, I had grown much less enthusiastic about teaching French to sullen and over-comfortable teenagers.

***

When I get into Hubert's skin as he stumbles along that track amongst the Waffen-SS, I feel loneliness. He is alone amongst all these men. There is no one to help him. I wonder if he ever realised the hopelessness of his

situation, the idea that he might not survive what little
was left of the day. Why had he been in the café at all?

His movements were simple and regular: he would
set off very early for the tannery, which was in St Maurice some seven kilometres away, on his bicycle or (if
the latter was needed by his mother) on foot, and work
until midday. Then he would eat his meagre lunch with
the other workers – all much older than himself. He
would be back in Valdaron by seven in the evening,
over twelve hours after he had set out. This would be
the pattern for five days of the week. On Saturdays, he
would return home at midday, which explains why he
could be in the café at five o'clock. Meanwhile, every
week in Valdaron, the silk factory (now derelict) would
flood the village street with its female workers both at
lunchtime and at the end of the afternoon – the noise
deafening as they sought their homes, the hooter sound-
ing over it all, each woman dressed in the factory's blue
overalls and the crowd resembling the unstoppable rush
of water. One of these women was Hubert's mother.

Hubert had worked at the tannery since he was
fourteen, and his clothes and hair and skin carried its
pungent smell. He had no brothers or sisters and his father was long dead, from delayed complications following a gas attack in Verdun. The boy remembered him as
stern and wheezing, but not so ill that he couldn't take
his son out hunting. On Sundays, Hubert would go to
church – not, like most of the village, to the Protestant

church at one end, but to the Catholic church on the main square.

The trouble with history is that it proliferates. You take one element and it leads to several others, all equally claiming your attention. How do we know that the men tipsy on Aimé's fig brandy weren't all Protestant, and suggested Hubert as a guide because he was Catholic? Believe it or not, this question obsessed me for a while. Perhaps this is because my own maternal family were Swedish Protestants of a particularly severe strain until my mother announced she was an atheist (and a Communist, to boot), while my father was a non-practising Jew who fled to Sweden from Estonia in 1940.

I have spent a lot of time, over the last twenty years, in and out of the archives, establishing the faiths of those I knew were present in the café that afternoon in 1944, but to no great conclusion.

I knew their names, of course, from the label on Aimé's bottle of fig brandy. And when I discovered, finally, how Hubert's body, with its shattered face, had lain on the track for three days before it was found by a shepherd, and then rested in a back room of the mairie at St Maurice for a further two days before a fellow tannery worker recognised the victim only by his withered hand, I was not surprised.

He had not been able to make the SS soldiers understand.

They were angry with him because the farmhouse was empty, although he knew nothing about it. They pushed him back down the track and then, two kilometres from the village, they shot him through the back of the head in cold blood.

Similarly, over the next twenty years, until it had grown into a life-crippling obsession, I would not be able to persuade anyone, however much I wheedled and cajoled, to tell me which among the owners of those scrawled names had suggested Hubert as a guide.

But now I have smashed the bottle. None of this matters any more. Now I can begin to live.

***

Before I returned to the area in 1989, I had never even heard of Hubert Cros; his was not one of the scribbled names.

I first saw it on a stone plaque set into a rock on a rough, wide track between the hills; I had walked up the track from the village, looking for a place to sling my hammock for the night. I almost missed the plaque, since it was the same colour as the rocks.

It stated that '*Ici*' — on this very spot! — '*le jeune Hubert Cros, agé de dix-neuf ans*' had been '*assassiné par les Nazis*' on 28th February, 1944. Of course, the date was the same as on the bottle. As I stared, aghast, I felt as if all my life had been a preparation for this meeting-point between three lives: mine, Hubert's, and Lucille's. I did not yet know that there was a fourth person involved, and that I was carrying his name in my rucksack.

I had by now moved to the Swedish part of Lapland to teach Russian and French in various schools spread over a considerable area; this was part of my idealism, to live in one of the remotest and most beautiful parts of Europe and submerge myself in the Sami way of life, which I regarded as one of the last 'native' cultures on the continent. Save yourself from the crowd, was my mantra. Follow your own drum. Do not be pushed along by the forces of conformism, of greed.

As it turned out, I was soon ground down by the difficulties of the job, by the truly terrible and overlong winters in which daylight is no more than a protracted delusion of the night, by the alcohol problems linked with hardship and loneliness and the sense that modern life was about to sweep the old ways into obliteration. Kiruna, after all, lives mostly by mining. Iron ore.

I spent much of my time driving in my 1940s Soviet Army jeep (which I had lovingly restored) to remote, shabby towns where the few pupils interested in either Russian or French had a certain sense of hopelessness behind their innate pride – their round, reddened faces turned towards me as if I might offer something more than grammatical rules, Molière and Pushkin. I think now that I was never a very good teacher, that it wasn't the Sami people's fault if I seemed to be getting nowhere; I began to feel I was part of the damage, as if modern schooling and health care and electricity and television were not the right of everyone, when really the damage was inside myself, because I had lost my way.

And I started to drink, like many of the locals I encountered.

Once the snow had begun properly to melt, I would take the jeep to a point marked on my hiking map and then I would stride out with my long legs, and soon I would lose any other walkers and be alone in the treeless wastes, the low mountains still with their snow on, the black lakes lapping at the pebbles in that very clear, cold light of spring. And, if it was summer, I would pitch a tent on some remote hill and watch the setting sun roll along the horizon, pausing as if to think about it and then rising again, sunset to dawn in three or four minutes, the gnats crowding around my face but rarely biting me because I had something natural in my sweat that they did not like.

Perhaps it was sugar, because sometimes I would drink myself into the ground, always with eau de vie, a very pure alcohol that damages you less than other spirits. I would wake up at some distance from my tent, with blood on my nose, as if something had struck me in the face when really it was the ground itself, and not know whether it was day or the middle of the night.

And once I dreamt, just before I came round with

my bloodied nose, that my face had been blown apart from behind by a bullet, a bullet fired at point-blank range into the back of my head and that had travelled on to emerge through my nostrils like a fist so that I was rendered unrecognisable.

A strange dream, marked by its precision of detail, its absolute thrill of gut fear. I took this dream to mean that I lacked an identity, that I did not know where I wanted to go, or what I wanted to be; all I knew was that I was perpetually dissatisfied with what was on offer, that the better world I had imagined was nowhere in sight, that all the minor irritations of life were tormenting me and hiding the great vistas and the golden light like the gnats in a black cloud around my head, and dragging me down. I would look at the lone bottle, back in my flat, and see again the dark, shining eyes of a girl teasing me to follow her into her life, and cry as Swedish men rarely cry – most of all this one.

And this is why I returned, thirteen years and a brief, unsatisfactory marriage later. I went all the way – from far above the Arctic circle to the southern heat – by train, carrying a rucksack in which the most precious item was an empty bottle scrawled over with names.

***

I hired a car, a little white Renault 4, at Nîmes station and I drove into the Cévennes mountains feeling nervous and excited and a disappointment to myself. The car was stiff and underpowered, and I would have preferred my long-ago mobilette because at least that had an eccentricity about it. Swedes are very cautious as well as thoughtful drivers – at least, they were in those days – and I found it hard to adapt to the French way. I was too used to my jeep, the bare wide spaces of Lapland, and by the time I saw the sign to Valdaron, I was feeling as if I had done a foolish thing, returning.

It was the summer, and very hot. The dryness in the air was not the same as the dry winter air of northern Sweden, it seemed to suck the damp from my insides. I loved it. The windows were down and I had already accustomed myself to that sweet, southerly perfume which makes me think of honey on toast or a girl's sun-warmed limbs.

I made it to Valdaron by six in the evening, on a thin thread of a road that wound tortuously between forest in which the cicadas could be heard warming up for the night chorus, even up here in the mountains. I would try to picture the village, as I lay in my bedroom in lonely Kiruna in the dead of winter, feeling depressed, with the snowlight glimmering on the dark-green glass of the bottle, and attempt to imagine how things might have been if I had said to Lucille, smiling at me and clearly fancying this tall Swede with the sun-burned face and sun-bleached hair: 'Can I buy you a coffee?'

And why the hell didn't I say that? Why the hell didn't I buy her a coffee and then help her pack up the stall at the end of the day and go for an evening walk and hold her hand and stroke her hair and kiss her, then kiss her again and so on? Why the hell not?

To that, I had no answer, even under the influence of eau-de-vie, even after my two years with Ulrike, a mild teaching-colleague who loved books. I was in the moment, back there in 1975, where I was too shy even to offer Lucille one of my unfiltered Gitanes – or maybe it actually never occurred to me to take my life in my own hands and jump. I might have ended up marrying her, living in Paris and coming down to see her family in the village. Or she might have accompanied me to Stockholm, where we would have started something together, not necessarily to do with France. An alternative cultural centre. A trendy bookshop, even. Or just worked in the same school together, teaching, our lives a perpetual love affair with each other, even when the beautiful kids came along. Was this what I saw in the genie's lamp of the bottle, without even rubbing it? The illusion that my life might not have been something of a shambles, necessarily? That Lucille wouldn't have found me as hard to live with, in my restlessness, as poor Ulrike did in spite of her books, her solid patience?

And then I would shake my head and realise that I had known Lucille for about ten minutes at the most. It was this very concentrated moment in my life, this white-heat moment, which had cooled and left a trace of glass that the grey snowlight of Lapland was now glimmering upon in my room in Kiruna. It was something more poetic than real. And yet somewhere inside it was a truth I couldn't grasp.

***

Valdaron hadn't changed much in thirteen years. It was like an Alpine village, I now realised: seaming a steep and narrow valley, only with red-ochre roofs instead of grey slate, and a rushing stream behind. The houses were still old, gaunt and peeling. There was a labyrinth of alleyways squeezed between the street and the river, but on the other side there was nothing but closed doors. It seemed narrower than I remembered it.

I parked the car and made for the exact spot in the square where Lucille had been with her stall, where I had first seen the bottle, where something had become deflected and led me, eventually, to regard myself as a disappointment. I couldn't stay long in that spot because they had recently cropped the plane trees and the sun was beating down on my head, but it made me think of how speedily time passes and with so little consideration for objective measurements, so that the bare paving stones where Lucille had sat behind the trestle were, although precisely the same (they have since been replaced with cobbles), only just vacated of her presence and at the same time erased entirely of her memory in some way, like preserved medieval towns that make you feel further from the Middle Ages than if you were sitting at home.

I decided to start with the café. Because it gave onto the street, there were no tables outside. The door stuck and I thought at first it was closed, but then I heard laughter from within. Instead of lifting the door slightly (it dragged on the linoleum), I pushed against the frame with some violence, with the help of my foot – ever the overlarge, clumsy Swede – and made quite a rumpus as I entered, the door's loose glass clattering.

The laughter had stopped. The silence was deepened by the noise that had preceded it.

My eyes adjusted to the gloom. There were a few old men around the corner table and one young man standing at the bar, all with their heads turned towards me as if I had dropped from Mars. I ordered a beer and a baguette sandwich from the taciturn barman, who had a large belly and heavy, stubbled jowls. It was slightly cooler inside, at least.

I was happy to be back in France: all this gritty reality was part of the experience. I got out my note-book and glanced at the page with the names, wondering whether to start my enquiries here. Perhaps I was a little fearful, but I needed to get going because it was early evening by now and I had no idea where I would be staying, although I had my hammock rolled up in the car so that all I needed was a couple of trees.

Instead – heart pounding, sweat beading on my brow – I asked about Lucille. 'Lucille Vilot?' She would be about thirty years old, perhaps early thirties?

The barman frowned, leaning on the zinc, and consulted the old men. There was no Lucille Vilot that they knew of. I said that maybe Vilot was not her name, but it was certainly that of her great-great-uncle, called Aimé. Great-great-uncle? I felt eccentric – an uncomfortable feeling for a Swede, even a Swede like me.

The young man spoke up. He was dressed in a workman's blue overalls, powdered here and there with sawdust. He looked about nineteen, with a clear, honest look in his eyes. I tried not to notice his hand, holding the cigarette between two scarred stumps. He said that would be Lucille Lacour, who had gone up to Paris with her husband a couple of years ago. He couldn't remember his name. The man was a lawyer, he added – with the hint of a grimace.

Was he sure of this?

'*Oui, monsieur.*'

I thanked him calmly, as if I didn't care very much either way, but one of the old men had come up to the bar and was looking at me with a twinkle in his eye.

'*Elle était mignonne*,' he declared, as the barman dried the glasses with a strange vigour. The old man's breath was sweet with spirits.

Yes, she was certainly *mignonne*, although I didn't like the term, it reduced her horribly. My face was reddening.

I paid hastily and left, burning with embarrassment. I fancied there was laughter again as I forced the door shut, but it might have been the rush of blood in my ears.

It was then, feeling as if my heart was a basket of eggs and that the bottom had fallen out of it, I decided to look for a place to sling my hammock before it grew too dark. I took all I needed from the car and found a wide track that climbed up from where a little hump-back bridge crossed the stream.

Of course she would have married and left! What the hell did I expect? That she'd be waiting for me?

I kept on walking, oblivious to my ostensible purpose, until I saw the plaque some two kilometres along the track, and blinked at the date chiselled upon it, scarcely believing my eyes.

I spent the night there, lying in my hammock in the trees a little way above the plaque and trying to sleep through the endless woodland rustlings and melancholy calls that seemed at one with my thoughts.

***

Today, however, I shot the bottle.

I am past fifty, I am now a school inspector, they are moving my town, and all this is over. Lucille, Hubert, Aimé – it is as if they never happened, swirled away into history. They have nothing to do with me, now. Not even the SS captain has anything to do with me, although I know that his grandson, sweet with expensive after-shave, is the director of a timber company logging illegally in Africa, and that his plump, friendly grandaughter has twins called Lili and Lena.

They are moving my town, lock stock and barrel; if not, Kiruna will sink further into the void left by the mining. It has been decided. One day we will all wake up with a different view, a different lake and forest and mountain.

So I sit in my doomed flat with its unceasing summer light that seems to roar at night behind my aluminium roll-down blinds, and no longer see the dark, shining eyes of the past. I am, in a way, free. It is just a question of making up for lost time, although I am honestly rather tired out, these days. I may even burn the notes I have accumulated, whole bundles of them, all the letters and their replies in coloured folders that have faded to similar shades on my shelves.

If I sleep, however, I may still dream in the same way. That will be interesting; to see if my dreams have stopped, at last. Or at least that particular dream, so vivid in its fear and pain.

I don't know anything about it, I always shout. *I don't know anything about it, I really don't!*

But it never makes any difference. They always laugh before finishing you off, thinking there is nothing you don't know.

The Numbers
Claire Wigfall

Numbers

ALL THAT I ken of numbers I learnt afore the age of 10. 1st on an abacus it was taught me, the instrument propped on the lady schoolteacher's desk. After, we progressed to numerals, copying the digits cannily on our slates with pieces of chalk, and rubbing at the answers with our sleeves if we made a miscalculation. The lot of us could fit on 2 benches at 1 time – wee 1s on 1 end, the seniors on the other. That's how wee the school is. Addition, subtraction, division, multiplication; I was always fond of numbers.

When I was 9 I received a prize for recitation of the multiplication tables: a gilt-edged book donated by a religious mission on the mainland. Spiritual Salvation the book was called. They kent we were a godless folk, but it didn't stop them trying. Faither placed the prize on the mantelshelf for safe keeping because we'd never had a book in the cottage afore and daren't to dirty the pages of this 1 by handling it, but after some time the soot from the fireplace clouded the paper dust-jacket black, and the heat made the cover-boards curl. You could say it was a shame, but the truth is there are worse things have happened in this world.

There were some on the island who wondered what we might need numbers for. These were the 1s who had never learnt to work with them in their day. They could count on their fingers if they were lucky, and hadn't ever felt lacking in their lives. They didn't approve of filling our heads with a subject so vague-like as numbers. Not that they'd say this afore the lady schoolteacher, mind, because she hailed of good family from the mainland; and besides, the woman was so awfy bonnie. Miss Galbraith was what she called herself, while the rest of us favoured identification through our faithers. Peigi daughter of Finlay is what they call me, Peigi NicFhionnlaigh. The women held their tongues in Miss Galbraith's presence and tried to affect that they were gentlewomen, and the men kept quiet altogether, which is a rare thing, I can tell you, and I believe was because they felt themselves abashed, she being that upon which they found themselves hankering when they awoke all feverish from a particular type of night-dream. (I ken this to be true because my brother Iain told it to me when he was 14.)

Thus it continued that the lady schoolteacher would

teach us numbers, and we'd learn them until we were 10 and it came time to leave the schoolhouse. And beyond that, apart from the odd occasion when you wanted to count out the eggs to bag up for the mainland, or read the clock perhaps, or work out how many ewes you'd lost in a sudden frost, you could say that numbers weren't of much use to us. Not practically speaking, that is. Which means that in the eyes of many there's little excuse for my fondness. Yet the way I view it, numbers lend a logic to the world. They explain things. Throw light upon problems and make you recognise truth. They can be a comfort.

Take, as example, the issue of marriage. There are 33 of us on the island, myself included. Of these, 6 are kin. Of the remaining 26 (I've subtracted myself), 10 are below the age of 15 and can thus be excluded. 8 remaining are male. 5 of these are wed already. 8 − 5 = 3. 3 unwed males above the age of 15, 1 of whom, it should be noted, is feeble-minded, 1 of whom is unreasonably ugly and kent for his crabbit temper, 1 of whom has been widowed already a good 4 decades, and all 3 of whom are owerly fond of whisky – although that last could be said of almost all the male folk on this island (some of the women folk, too), so perhaps shouldn't be held against them. But you grant where the arithmetic is leading me?

Which is the beauty of numbers. They lay down the facts with such plainness and order you realise it's simply not worth upsetting yourself ower. Even if the solution isn't quite to your liking, in the end it is just a question of arithmetic. Simple arithmetic. Numbers. And who would be foolish enough to rail against numbers?

Boots

When I was 7 and a G a team of men came to our island. They were from a place called Cambridge, they told us, which is in England. We kent about England from the geography instruction the lady schoolteacher had learnt us. We kent our country was divided into 4, and that England was down near the bottom and that they have such things as motorcars there, which are vehicles rather like a dray but which can move of their own accord.

These men wore their face hair clipped into neat shapes and had coloured belts of silk tied about their necks and spoke to 1 another in a language we couldn't understand.

They walked across to the north side of the island and erected a wee canvas tent beside the blackened tarry limb that our men had uncovered some 2 seasons back while cutting peat, and left untouched out of deference to a body taken afore his time.

I have told you we are not a religious folk, and believe not in the existence of gods in the sky above, but there is not 1 child on this island who does not ken of the darksome boggarts who lie beneath us. They bide in the peat bogs, and are looking for any opportunity they can to lay their fingers upon life and pull it to the depths they do inhabit. They are clever, we are told, sleekit with it, and on foggy nights they have been kent to call in thin voices to those they wish to lure unto them. Men, walking home late of an evening, tight after a few drams of whisky, have heard the voices of young lassies calling to them from the fog. Tempting them with that which they desire. It takes a steely heart to walk by.

I once saw a bull that had stumbled into a bog. It was sunk neck-deep already by the time it was found, and was slipping deeper so very slowly it almost looked as if it wasn't going anywhere. It took 8 men to haul the creature out, their ropes looped about his horns.

These men from England did not own the caution of our menfolk. They set about the peat with metal tools and scrapers and eventually were able to lift a body from the clutches of the dank soil once liquidy enough to drown this poor soul. We islanders were allowed to observe their prize. It looked asleep, its spine curved like the line of a ram's horn and the knees pulled up against the chest. The skin was a horrid black-broon with a silver-grey shine to it, and drooped upon the bones beneath like the flesh of a fruit that has turned. The hair was red-broon, but without any shine, like a hank of wool afore it has been spun. Upon its feet remained a pair of leather boots, black-broon like the rest of the body.

I stood afore the trestle table and stared and stared. We had been instructed not to touch. The adults too, as if they were children needed learning. So I don't ken what came ower me, but the truth is there are instances when you are propelled by possibilities you might ken are without reason. I moved my hand swiftly, as if it were a dare made to me by Iain or Mairead. As quickly again my faither slapped my hand away. 'You think you'd like it?' he scolded. 'To be stared at like that? And then prodded by a horrid wee lassie?' And he cuffed my ear sharply as if I deserved the blame for everyone's curiosity.

Herrings

Each January sees the beginning of the herring season. Salt herring is what we eat most nights, alongside tatties, and is responsible, some say, for the stomach crampings so many of us suffer from. The drifters from the mainland ports return laden with catches of the fish that must be gutted and packed in barrels of salt for export.

If the north wind is not too squally, a boat is sent ower and us girls, or those that can be spared, go athwart to help with the gutting.

Ower a decade now I have been aiding at the gutting, and yet I still have not found my sea legs. I am afeared of the water, and confess the journey is a torment for me, with the boat tipping us this way and that, and myself praying my stomach shan't pitch my breakfast porridge ower the edge.

Last year was no exception. I left the cottage afore sunrise, and walked 4 miles in lantern-light to reach the beachfront. I couldn't help but count the steps down to the shore, and told myself that if the final tally was even, the journey athwart the water would not drown us. The final step was odd. But then I considered the return journey I would have to make that night, and agreed with myself that I could factor this into the sum, allowing me to multiply the number by 2. After that I felt much more at ease.

3 other girls were waiting already, their faces pinched against the cauld and drizzle, their shawls wrapped tightly around them. The bonnie sisters Anna and Caìtriona NicPhàdraig were there. And young Màiri, daughter of Alasdair the fiddler, who was joining us for her 1st gutting. Maureen NicAindreas, Domhnall MacAindreas's feeble-minded sister, was absent. We all agreed this was for the best, considering the incident at the previous year's gutting. It had been discomfiting for all involved. Besides, Maureen had been laid poorly for some time and we none of us had seen too much of her for a while.

We shared some pleasantries, and in the gloaming of the early dawn saw the rowboat coming towards us athwart the waves.

***

You will imagine my surprise when I found I recognised the fellow at the tiller. Willeam MacGhobain, who studied in the schoolhouse with me. I remembered him a bone-pale timid laddie, who caught the croup when he was 13 and was sent ower to his aunt on the mainland where he could be nursed in the hospital. A few of the other schoolchildren used to take a rise out of me on occasions, once or twice driving me into quite a temper, saying that Willeam held something of a fancy for me. But after leaving us, he never returned to the island, and I had not spared him too much thought in the years that had past.

With the oars in his gloved hands, he was still pale as I remembered him, but harsh winds and cauld weather had thickened his skin. He had a long sheepish face now, with yellow hair sticking which-way from his crown. Even his eyebrows and lashes were yellow. He lifted a hand to help each 1 of us into the boat, and as he took my own and looked up at me I saw recollection flash athwart his face. To my great shame, he blushed like a lassie.

I dipped my head as I took my seat and let go his hand quickly, but out of the corner of my eye I could see the red flushing at his cheekbones and creeping along the curlicues of his ears. 'Why,' I thought to myself, 'he is just as foolish as ever he was.'

'Willeam MacGhobain?' I said to him, hoping the other girls had paid no heed to his colouring. 'It is a full 14 years since we saw each other last, is it not?' Which meant that I had not kent him for 1 full year longer than I had kent him, so really I did not ken him very well at all.

The others in the boat were a good deal younger than us, and thus had never afore seen Willeam in their lives, but we 2 spoke as he pulled us athwart the grey water.

'You are not married?' he asked, for married women do not so normally go athwart to the gutting.

I replied that I was quite content as I was, and very busy with it. My faither would surely not get by without me now our mother was gone. I explained that Iain had taken ower the croft, and had a cottage nearby with his wife and their 3 young 1s.

'And you had a sister,' he said.

'We lost Mairead,' I told him, but did not feel able to say more on that matter. Besides, the wind was up, and the tipping of the boat was rather beginning to affect me. I took a deep breath to steady my wits, and as solace reminded myself that the number of steps had come out even. Then I counted 8 a few times in my head, for good measure. Anna and Caitriona were singing – a hearty sea ballad – and I wondered how they could manage it. 'You must have a wife and family, no doubt,' I ventured, so he wouldn't think me snubbing him, 'ower on the mainland?'

Now it was his turn to look away, and for the wind I barely heard him tell me that his wife had passed.

He came at the end of the day and took us home. 'You will come again tomorrow, Peigi NicFionnlaigh?'

'I daresay,' I told him. 'And you will row the boat, Willeam MacGhobain?'

'I daresay,' he replied with a smile.

I tried not to think about that smile on my walk home. The fog had crawled in, and the path was hard to see, even in the light of my lantern. It is dangerous to let your concentration slip on such a night. But I found my mind turning ower the things that he had told me, and imagining his life on the mainland, living in that tall brick house with his 2 wee motherless bairns and his maiden aunt who was suffering so now from arthritis. So occupied was my mind, I almost didn't hear the voice in the fog.

At 1st I thought it a wee beastie. A lamb that had got lost, perhaps, and was greiting for its mammy. But it wasn't the lambing season. I held up my lantern in the rainy mist and listened. I ventured the sound could be far off perhaps, carried on the fingers of the wind. There was naught to be seen beyond the yellow halo the fog made about my lantern. Again came the sound. A thin, eerie wail. A chill shivered through my bones and my breath quite stopped.

I listened, and now I could hear nothing beside the wind howling athwart the treeless land. 'You're letting your foolish imagination carry you away, Peigi daughter of Finlay,' I told myself sharply, and turning back to the path took a few hurried steps, wanting to be home and in the warm, cooking up the herrings in my bag for Faither. But then it came again. Closer this time it seemed, or louder at least. A sound quite aching with loneliness.

My feet halted. 'You silly creature, ignore it,' I said out loud. 'It is nothing but the call of the darksome boggarts trying to trick you. Walk on. Walk on, you foolish girl!' But my heart would not allow it. The thin cry I heard in the darkness touched a deep and trembly chord inside me, and against all sense and reason I could nay ignore it.

Each step I took from the path was made cannily, 1 toe feeling ahead to confirm solid ground, and betwixt each step I paused to listen for the sound. Sometimes, it seemed louder, at others it would hush completely. 'Helloo?' I called into the night. 'Be anyone there?' But the wind seemed to carry my words instantly up and away into the dark sky.

I had taken 8 paces 3 times ower into a fog that closed behind me with each step I took, and kent that the further I went, the harder it would be to find my way back. I confess I was just about to gather my senses and turn around again when I saw in the lantern light a dim pale shape on the ground before me. Silly thing that I am, it made me leap. I thought it perhaps a wraith, crouching before it jumped at me, but the shape did not move. I daresay I have never felt so afeared in my life. But I had come this far, and kent I could nay turn back. I knelt carefully, set my lantern upon the gorse, and inched my hand forwards through the dense fog. What my cauld fingers touched was a rough woollen blanket, the oldest blanket you could imagine. All torn and dirtied and studded with burrs as if it had lined a cowshed. I pulled back 1 corner and that which I found made me gasp. This was no spectre beneath my fingertips. No darksome boggart. No wraith. This was flesh and blood.

Disturbed by the icy draft, the wee infant began again at its greiting.

Potatoes

When my grandmother was a wee lassie, a blight turned the potatoes soft. She could recall helping her parents to pull them from the earth. Tattie after tattie, each 1 shrivelly and threaded with rot. They sorted throu gh them to see if any could be salvaged, then collected the rest into a pile in 1 corner of the croft and left them there. Her parents talked of quitting the island, of taking a boat as others were doing far athwart the seas to a land called Canadia. But our family have lived on this island for generations, and my grandmother's elders were not certain they could conceive of a life beyond it.

She was never schooled, my grandmother. The schoolhouse was closed for cause of the blight. It was not a time for education, and besides, the children of the island were too weak to walk all that way each day. Thus she never learnt about arithmetic, she never learnt how to read a page from a book, she never learnt geography, she never even learnt to write her name. But my grandmother could sing. Even in later years her voice was clear and tempered like the movement of water through a burn. 'Ach, I filled my empty stomach with song,' she told me, explaining how she survived when so many others did not.

There were lullabies she used to sing to me, songs that had been sung to her by her own mother, and that she had sung to my mother afore me. I remember lying beneath the blankets in the same bed I sleep in now but at that time shared with Iain and Mairead. I can recall with great clarity the crackle of the fire and the sound of my grandmother's voice as I fought to keep my eyes from drooping.

***

I sang those same lullabies to the baby, and they seemed to soothe her. 'Hee balou,' I hushed. 'Hee balou.' So wee was she. So very fragile I feared she might break. The dome of her head pressed slightly, it was not firm like my own, and the broon hair was like the softest down you can imagine.

At 1st Faither wanted naught to do with her. He told me to take her back out again and leave her where I'd found her, but I told him straight I would do nothing of the sort, and in the end he had to let it be for he could see I was full determined, and he is an old man now, and no longer as strong as he once was. I told him to banish his ridiculous fancies from his head and fill the biggest cooking pot we had with water and warm it on the fire.

She was wee enough to fit right in the pot, and I joked that she could make a bonnie stew. Faither laughed at that. He hadn't had his herrings yet and I daresay he was awfy hungry. All the while, as he helped to scoop the water ower her, I was taking care to hold her safely, and support her head. I was not used to holding such a wee infant, especially when slippery with water and soap. I counted each finger and toe, and all was perfect. 'She is not long of this world,' Faither told me. 'Only a day or so, I would venture.'

As we were drying her afore the fire, she started again to whimper and we agreed she must be hungry, so while I wrapped her in a pillowslip and then the softest blanket I could find, Faither went out and fetched a cup of milk from the cow. I used my little finger and a silver teaspoon to drip it in her mouth and it seemed to calm her until eventually she fell to sleep in my arms.

'You will have to cook the herrings,' I told Faither. 'For I don't think I can move.'

Superstitions

For sure all folk ken that 2 crows flying ower a house foretells a wedding, or that a grave dug on a Sunday will lead to another being dug for the body's kin afore the week is out, or that a slip of rowan tied with a red thread and kept on 1's person on the eve afore May Day will be a charm against ill luck and avert evil from 1's flocks and herds. We grow up with these superstitions. We learn them afore we even ken they are being taught. We all put on our right shoes 1st of a morning without ever asking ourselves why.

It is bad luck to let the moon shine on an infant's face, or to have them sleep in a new cradle. Their clothes should be passed through a fire, and a dobbet of butter should be dropped in their mouth and swallowed if they are to be protected from malignant spirits.

I did all that which I could for her.

But still my brother Iain warned, 'Peigi, folk will not take well to that bairn. Not when you found her in the mist like you did, with no indication of where she might hail from, and that blush you won't acknowledge upon her face. There is some darksome magick surrounding her and she'll bring bad luck to the island, that's what they will say. I turned from him and walked back alone to the cottage, holding the baby close against my chest.

They came to look her ower. I kent they would. And of course I could not turn them away from the door, that would not be proper. We went flat through our supply of tea-leaves, and my arm was quite aching from the pouring of whisky. I cooked butter-saps in the pan, always a dainty at a new birth, until we were out of oatmeal.

Out of politeness they kept their tongues quiet, but I saw the looks between them, and when I quit the room to check on her, lying in the cradle begged from Iain and his wife, the walls weren't thick enough to block out the speculatings Iain had predicted. To drown their words I counted 8 ower and again. I did look hard at her bonnie wee face, but I could see no darksome magick.

Domhnall MacAindreas even came to our door, and he has certainly never shown interest in a bairn afore. There is little amity shared between the 2 of us, and never has been. A rough, ugly man, with a temper to match. His horrid eyes have a way of lingering on your flesh.

'Folk are saying you've found a bairn out in the fog, Peigi NicFhionnlaigh, with the markings of the Deil upon its gruntle, isn't that so? I thought I'd better come and have a wee look.'

'Are you sure it's not our whisky bottle you are wanting a wee look at, Domhnall MacAindreas?'

'Ach, but I'll be wanting a look at that too, for sure I will. But 1st this bairn.' And he stepped inside without even wiping his boots.

I didn't like his manner, but I felt obliged to show him through to the bedroom. As he pulled back the coverlet from her chin with his hairy fat fingers, a crabbit look came upon his face. I had to halt myself from spitting at my handkerchief to rush and wipe at her cheek where he had touched.

'Oh, but Peigi NicFionnlaigh,' he said unpleasantly, 'no good will come of this 1. No good at all.'

I didn't see this to be a comment fit for reply.

I cleared 9 plates and 12 glasses and 2 spent whisky bottles at the end of the night, and found just 1 glass unemptied. The wee 1 Mother used to favour, with a lick of blue paint around its rim. It was the glass that Domhnall MacAindreas had been sipping from. That man has nay been kent to leave even a single drop at the bottom of his whisky glass, so I kent he'd done so out of spite. For all folk ken that it is dangerous to the health of a newborn bairn not to finish your glass.

I had missed 1 full week of the gutting. And as I walked again athwart the hills I realised I had not thought once about Willeam MacGhobain. In fact, it seemed a lifetime now since that morning when I'd 1st climbed into his boat and said helloo. I wondered if he had noted my absence.

As I drew closer to the beachfront, I began to grow

apprehensive, and had to count 8 for a while. The others surely would have spoken to him already. I had to stop myself from running the last stretch because I wanted to grab him and shout, 'No, none of it's true. She's nay bad luck, that's foolish talk. There's naught unnatural or darksome about her. She's beautiful. Beautiful. You'd ken it too if you could see her!'

But to my shock, as I took his hand and climbed into the boat, I didn't see that look of discomfit that I expected. Instead he smiled, that halting smile of his, and asked me what I'd called her.

'Sine,' he repeated after me, as if he wanted to taste the sound of the word in his mouth. It is our word for gift.

'Sine,' I replied.

Milk

He came on a gustery afternoon.

I was alone with her, Faither having gone up on the croft to help Iain with a sickly ewe. The sky was greying up outside, and I'd been forced to light the lamp. I had a batch of wool for carding, but 1st wanted to set a pan of milk on the fire to warm because I could tell she'd be getting hungry. You would not believe how she had grown. How healthy the wee creature was looking.

The shock of him banging at the door like that caused me to spill the milk all ower the hearthstones. Like a madman he was banging, and a moment later he came storming through the door, letting in the wind and the cauld with him. 'Where be the bastard?' he roared. 'Where is it hiding?'

I have never seen a man so filled with fury. His eyes were blazing with it, and it seemed to charge the air about him. He burst into our wee living room afore I could say a word. Cursing, he knocked against the side table, and in his anger hurled it athwart the room so it broke in 2. His hair was all uncombed, and he was reeking of drink, his breath dank with it. Unwashed he was too. I could smell the sweat and grease of him, like the wool afore it has been soaked. He was like a man possessed, not seeing of me at all, just focused on his purpose. His voice was raging and his words coarser than any I'd ever heard spoken by any man.

They asked me later why I did nothing, but what they don't understand is that it all happened so fast.

He saw the basket beside the fire and grabbed for her, his hairy fingers snatching her from the cushions and shaking the poor thing as if she were little more than a sack of potatoes.

I did cry out. That I did. But his arm smacked me sharply around the head so I fell hard against the wall, and by the time I had arisen he was already out the door again.

I ran straight after them, hollering at him to let me have her back, but he is a big man, Domhnall MacAindreas, and more than once he sent me reeling. I was like the irritation of a fly to him, easily swatted away.

I could not catch him, even stumbling as he was for all the drink in him. And I tell you how I did try. I grabbed at his shirtsleeves, and caught a lock of his hair, and clung on 1 leg even, afore he kicked me away. I did try to stop him, harder than anything afore in my life.

But then it happened.

When I look again upon it now, in my dreams, in the recollections they forced from me, I see it all occur so slowly. It can nay have been that way, but certainly it was time enough for all colour to drain from my face. He appeared just to wobble backwards a moment on the dry gorse, his arm lifting as he did, and then he let her go and hurled her in a steep arc through the air. Where she fell, the lace coverlet she'd been wrapped in trailed milken athwart the black surface of the peat bog.

'Bastard,' he cried, stumbling, his legs criss-crossing and threatening to topple him. 'Bastard, be gone with ye,' he cursed.

I lost my senses, I'll confess it now. When they pulled me from the bog, my skirts and hands and hair heavy with the thick black sludge, Iain had to slap me about the cheek afore I was able to collect myself again and see the matter straight. There is no use greiting ower spilt milk, was what my mother used to say.

Porridge

I went again this year to the gutting, and again Willeam MacGhobain was at the tiller.

'Greetings to you, Peigi NicFionnlaigh,' he said to me, with a short smile of sadness.

'Greetings, Willeam MacGhobain,' I replied.

The sickness started almost as soon as we pulled away from the shore, and I closed my eyes, feeling sure that this time my breakfast porridge would not have the strength to stay fast.

We did not speak either of us on the journey ower, and I believe it was because he did not ken what words to say to me. But on our return he touched my knee with his fingers as the oar stroked past, and said, 'Why do you count like that, Peigi NicFionnlaigh?'

'Pardon?' I replied, for it took me a moment to work his meaning.

'No,' he said with a shake of his head, 'no matter.' He gave me a smile. 'I heard you were ower on the mainland a few months back.'

'That's correct,' I replied plainly. 'And I don't think I'd be wanting to return. All those folk and filth. I can nay ken how you suffer it.' It had been the 1st time I'd ever ventured beyond the herring yard.

He tipped his head, and I saw the cauldness of my words had hurt him. He always was a soft lad. 'Well, at least it looks as though the trial will reach its proper conclusion,' he said thinly.

'It looks that way.'

He pulled a few more strokes, his mouth tight, his eyes not looking in my direction. I felt suddenly sorry for how I'd treated him, when he was showing only kindness. But I didn't ken how to right it.

'To think that he'd been doing such wicked things with his poor simple sister,' said I. I had to swallow hard, and for sure it must have been the tipping of the boat.

The numbers wouldn't stay straight, they kept jumbling as I tried to order them.

Out of the corner of my eye, I glanced his way again and saw that he was watching me sadly, while his fine strong hands pulled the oars through the dark water.

I felt the lurching of my stomach, and thought how ugly I must look, green with the desire to vomit. My hands reeked of fish guts and salt and harsh carbolic soap. For a moment I thought how easy it might be to simply tip back ower the edge of the boat and sink beneath the grey waves.

But of course now, that would have been against reason.

Biographical Notes

RICHARD BEARD was born in Swindon in 1967. His first published story, 'The Three Rope Trick', appeared in the fiction magazine *Panurge* in 1994, and since then he has published one further story, 'Hearing Myself Think', in *Prospect* and *New Writing* 15 (2007). In 1994 he enrolled on Malcolm Bradbury's Creative Writing MA at the University of East Anglia, and has published four novels including *X 20 A Novel of (not) Smoking* (1996), *Dry Bones* (2004), and *Damascus* (1999), a *New York Times* Notable Book of the Year.

He has also written three works of non-fiction, and *Muddied Oafs, The Last Days of Rugger* (2003) was shortlised for the British Sports Book Awards. His latest book, *Becoming Drusilla* (2008), is the biography of his friendship with the illustrator Dru Marland, and their eventful walking trip around Wales after Dru changed sex

Between 2003 and 2006 Richard Beard was Visiting Professor at the University of Tokyo. He currently lives in Strasbourg.

JANE GARDAM is the only writer to have been twice awarded the Whitbread prize for Best Novel of the Year (for *The Queen of the Tambourine* and *The Hollow Land*). She also holds a Heywood Hill Literary Prize for a lifetime's contribution to the enjoyment of literature. Her novel, *God on the Rocks,* was shortlisted for the Booker Prize and made into a film, while her collection of short stories have won many awards, including the David Higham Award and the Royal Society of Literature's Winifred Holtby Prize (for *Black Faces, White Faces*); the Katherine Mansfield Prize (for *The Pangs of Love*); and the Macmillan Silver PEN Award (for *Going Into a Dark House*). *Old Filth* was shortlisted for the Orange Prize 2005.

Born in Yorkshire, Jane Gardam is married with three grown-up children. She lives in Sandwich, Kent.

ERIN SOROS was born in Vancouver, British Columbia, Canada, where she worked as a rape crisis counsellor and coordinator of literacy programs for marginalised youth. She has published poetry, fiction and non-fiction, most recently in the *Indiana Review*, the *Iowa*

Review and the in-flight magazine *enRoute*. Her stories have been produced for the radio by the CBC and BBC as recipients of the CBC Literary Award and the Commonwealth Prize for the Short Story. She is the winner of the 2007 Charles Pick Fellowship at the University of East Anglia.

Poet, playwright and novelist ADAM THORPE was born in Paris in 1956 and grew up in India, Cameroon and England. After graduating from Magdalen College, Oxford, in 1979, he started a theatre company and toured villages and schools before moving to London where he taught Drama and English Literature. His first collection of poetry, *Mornings in the Baltic* (1988), was shortlisted for the Whitbread Poetry Award. His other books of poetry are *Meeting Montaigne* (1990), *From the Neanderthal* (1999), *Nine Lessons From the Dark* (2003) and *Birds With A Broken Wing* (2007). He was awarded an Eric Gregory Award in 1985.

Thorpe's first novel, *Ulverton* (1992), a panoramic portrait of English rural history, was published to great critical acclaim and prompted novelist John Fowles, reviewing the book in the *Guardian,* to call it 'the most interesting first novel I have read these last years'. The book consists of 12 loosely-connected narrative episodes tracing 350 years in the history of a rural village and its inhabitants, employing various narrative forms from dense prose written in thick dialect to modern film script. The book won the Winifred Holtby Memorial Prize in 1992.

His second novel, *Still* (1995), follows film director Ricky Thornby's ambitious plans to make an all-encompassing film about the twentieth century. *Pieces of Light* (1998), describes a young boy's childhood in West Africa and the mystery that develops when he is sent to live with an eccentric uncle in the English countryside on the eve of the Second World War. *Shift,* (2000), a collection of short stories, explores the interconnected themes of work and labour. *Nineteen Twenty-One* (2001), set in that year, focuses on a young man intent on writing a novel about the First World War. *No Telling* (2003), is set in 1968 and is narrated by a 12-year-old boy on the verge of First Communion and puberty, living amid a deeply dysfunctional family in a turbulent France, culminating in the 1968 Paris riots. *The Rules of Perspective* (2005), is set at the end of the Second World War in a German museum. *Between Each Breath* (2007), is a love story, following Jack Middleton, once a promising young composer and now living comfortably in Hampstead with his wife Milly, and the effects of the affair he had in Estonia with the beautiful Kaja six years before. Adam's forthcoming novel, *The Standing Pool*, follows the Mallinsons as they take a sabbatical in a remote Languedoc farmhouse, and is published by

Jonathan Cape in June 2008. *Is This The Way You Said?* (2006), is his most recent collection of stories.

Adam Thorpe lives in France with his wife and three children.

CLARE WIGFALL was born in Greenwich, London, during the summer of 1976. Her family moved to Berkeley, California in 1979 before returning to the UK when Clare was eight. She began writing at an early age and a few years later began working as assistant and editor to the late President of Mensa. After graduating from Manchester University in 1998, Clare moved to Prague and she now lives in Berlin. Her stories have been published in *Prospect*, *New Writing 10*, *Tatler*, the *Dublin Review*, and also commissioned for Radio 4.